A Candlelight Ecstasy Romance

"WHEN I SEE SOMETHING I WANT, I GET IT," JOE MURMURED.

"And I want you. I want to hold you, take care of you, make love to you." His strong arms came around her, pulling her close. "You're mine now, Gilly. And I'll never let you go."

Gilly felt herself grow tense in his arms. "Joe, I'm not a child to protect and take care of. You—you sound so possessive. . . ."

"That's the way it should be," he insisted, staring into her eyes with a look of bold desire. "A woman is meant to be loved, cherished, protected."

And suddenly he was kissing her passionately. Gilly felt herself melt in his arms, but she could not escape her nagging fears. Was Joe Bennett too much man for her to handle? Was he determined to take possession of her and of her life?

CANDLELIGHT ECSTASY ROMANCES®

WITH A
LITTLE LOVE

Natalie Stone

A CANDLELIGHT ECSTASY ROMANCE®

Published by
Dell Publishing Co., Inc.
1 Dag Hammarskjold Plaza
New York, New York 10017

Dell ® TM 681510, Dell Publishing Co., Inc.

Candlelight Ecstasy Romance®, 1,203,540, is a registered
trademark of Dell Publishing Co., Inc., New York, New York.

ISBN: 0-440-19546-2

Printed in the United States of America

July 1986

10 9 8 7 6 5 4 3 2 1

WFH

To Our Readers:

We have been delighted with your enthusiastic response to Candlelight Ecstasy Romances®, and we thank you for the interest you have shown in this exciting series.

In the upcoming months we will continue to present the distinctive, sensuous love stories you have come to expect only from Ecstasy. We look forward to bringing you many more books from your favorite authors and also the very finest work from new authors of contemporary romantic fiction.

As always, we are striving to present the unique, absorbing love stories that you enjoy most—books that are more than ordinary romance.

Your suggestions and comments are always welcome. Please write to us at the address below.

Sincerely,

The Editors
Candlelight Romances
1 Dag Hammarskjold Plaza
New York, New York 10017

WITH A
LITTLE LOVE

CHAPTER ONE

"Anything! I'll take *anything*. Just gas one up and let me get going!" Joe Bennett rubbed his shoulders through his plaid shirt, trying to ease the tight strain in his muscles.

"I'm very sorry, Mr. Bennett. I put the order for the van in yesterday, just as soon as your secretary called. I don't know why there's been this delay. Certainly we'll make some adjustment on the cost, throw in a set of floor mats, a tank of gas—"

"Forget it," Joe snapped, the words chipping a momentary break in the thin, straight line of his lips. His mouth looked as if it were made for laughter, for smiling, but this afternoon he couldn't think of a thing to smile about.

Drumming his fingers on the salesman's desk he cut off the man's apologies. "Look, I need that van *now*. I'm already running late!"

The small towheaded boy standing beside him seemed oblivious to his father's mood. Hands shoved in blue pants and obviously proud of the crisp yellow cub neck-erchief tied around his neck, the young boy let his eyes dance from one luxurious van to another while the sales-man's solicitous voice droned on.

"Mr. Bennett, I'll get a van immediately. I'm terribly sorry for this inconvenience."

The salesman backed out of the tiny office that seemed impossibly filled with Joe's angry height, turned on his heel, and fled. Joe shouldered the camping gear that had been tossed beside the door, followed him through the showroom and out onto the lot, his son scurrying to keep up.

Casting a quick glance around, Joe pointed to a nearby van. "That one." His eyes shifted downward to the boy. "You like the color, Adam?"

Adam nodded enthusiastically.

"Okay, we'll take it."

"Shall I clean it up?"

Joe snapped open the door, scooped the eight-year-old up into a passenger's seat, and climbed inside himself. He thrust out his hand for the keys. "Don't bother. Where I'm going, it won't make a bit of difference."

With a broad, powerful hand, a hand bare of rings or watch, tanned dark by a long summer of tennis and swimming, Joe gripped the gearshift and sent the van nosing into traffic.

It was four o'clock on a Friday, and the Philadelphia streets were clogged with motorists and buses and hurry-ing pedestrians. Everyone was rushing somewhere: home, to the bars, to Atlantic City and the casinos, to a last weekend fling before the weather turned mean.

Not that it mattered much, Joe thought. *He* felt mean already. It had been that kind of week. A series of bugs in the new program for IBM had kept him locked in the office for days, leaving no time for running, or laps, or even a pickup game of racket ball early in the mornings. And he was sure as hell feeling it now!

Again he shrugged at the tension in his back and shoulders, and ran a hand through the thick, dark hair that fell over his forehead. A kid on a bicycle cut suddenly across traffic, and Joe's hands gripped the steering wheel until his knuckles whitened beneath the force. The blare of his horn joined the shrill cacophony of horns around him.

Damn! Why didn't someone teach that kid some safety rules? Don't they cover that in school, or at home? The biker looked about thirteen . . . and he could have been killed. *Dead before he had a chance to live.* Memory gripped Joe with steely fingers and a shiver walked up his spine.

He shook away the old feelings and looked over his shoulder at Adam, settled safe and contented in the roomy back captain's chair. The boy had discovered the luxury van's small television set and was totally wrapped up in an old Pink Panther movie. He hadn't even been aware of the close call, Joe thought, his face softening.

He's quite a kid, he mused, with the first hint of a smile softening his face. Even at eight it was clear how bright Adam was, how eager to learn and do and . . . and how eager to please.

Joe swallowed, his throat suddenly dry. Then why did he always get the feeling that Adam was just a little afraid of him? No, not afraid; it wasn't that bad, just a little standoffish, a little withdrawn, since the divorce. But Joe had spent the last six years taking damn good care of the boy, making sure he was safe and well and protected. He'd spared him all the arguments, the painful discussions. The things that left scars on kids. He'd built a good life for Adam. A *safe* life. Nothing would ever hurt his son—Joe Bennett would see to that.

Joe shook his head, the noise of the traffic suddenly

11

deafening, his head pounding as though someone were punching computer keys right above his eyes. The back of his neck ached, and the grayness of the afternoon perfectly matched his mood.

Lifting one hand from the wheel he wiped his palms against the thighs of his jeans, then glanced at the mimeographed paper from Adam's den mother. They were almost at the Hickory Hills Elementary School, meeting point for this grand overnight excursion that Adam had cajoled him into.

No, Joe amended with a flash of guilt, he hadn't really been cajoled; he had *wanted* to go on the camp-out—at least theoretically. He needed time like that with Adam, time away from the telephone and computers and the sundry other things that so often fogged his mind and diverted his attention from his son. He had read all the books; he knew! One on one—that's what growing kids needed.

Several drops of rain scooted across the windshield as Joe pulled the van into the large asphalt parking lot adjacent to the school. *Gray,* he thought, his dark brows drawing into the frown he wore so often now; *another gray, miserable day.*

And then he saw her, like a sudden ray of sunshine.

She was standing at the edge of the parking lot in the middle of a straggly group of blue-shirted boys, all vying for her attention. Her slender frame rose above the circle of freckle-faced eight-year-olds and seemed to bristle with kinetic energy. In what seemed to be one motion she straightened a cub's necktie, pulled a leaf from another boy's hair, tugged her own honey-blond hair free of her collar, and pointed up at a squirrel scolding in the tree above. She never stopped smiling.

"It's Mrs. Holmes!" Adam shrieked in his ear, noticing his whereabouts for the first time. Joe stared. So this was Gilly Holmes, Adam's much-talked-about den mother.

She seemed barely to notice as the van pulled closer, so intent was she on the gaggle of grinning faces looking up at her. Satisfied after counting heads she shoved her hands into the pockets of her well-worn jeans and turned her gaze to Joe as he edged the van into a parking spot and Adam Bennett jumped out and joined the waiting group of boys.

Joe followed slowly. The misty gray day lightened, and as he neared Gilly Holmes, Joe Bennett felt the tension and pain of work and worry drain from his body. Interest, of a definitely sensual nature, took its place.

The woman was lovely. Lovely in an arty sort of way, with that thick hair framing delicately carved cheekbones and her slender body comfortably encased in faded jeans and cotton shirt. She had blue eyes—the blue of the sky right after rain.

Adam looked at his father as the tall man strode up beside him. The young boy's voice quieted to a respectful whisper. "Dad, here she is." His gaze shifted to Gilly's face and a shy smile fell into place. He touched his father's arm hesitatingly. "This is my den leader, Dad. Mrs. Holmes, this is . . . this is my dad." His small hand drifted down to his side.

Gilly grinned affectionately at Adam. "So this is your father, Adam. Wonderful!" Her eyes drew upward. "Hello, I'm Gilly Holmes. It's nice to meet you, Mr. Bennett."

"Joseph Bennett. Joe." He smiled now, slowly, and Gilly saw the shadow of a dimple flash quickly, then disappear in his left cheek.

Adam's description of his father—"He's old and works hard . . . but he just *loves* to camp, Mrs. Holmes!"— certainly hadn't prepared Gilly for the six-foot-two figure standing so close to her she could feel his body heat in the crisp autumn air.

The right side of her artist's mind quickly registered

the strong planes of his facial bones that made him, although not classically handsome, very interesting-looking. The kind of man she enjoyed watching from the secluded safety of a shadowed park bench or in a crowd of people at the bus stop. She frowned slightly, realizing with a start that her brain had already etched into memory the thick eyebrows and strong nose, the deep, thoughtful eyes, the slightly curved, sensuous lips of Joe Bennett's face. A good face for a charcoal sketch, drawn in dark, decisive strokes. A face that would perhaps appear again in her thoughts, bidden or not.

The feeling that his dark eyes were reading her thoughts brought her back to reality quickly. "Well, Joe, it's nice to meet you. And I can't tell you how much I appreciate your helping out with this camp-out." There, the control was back in her voice. She laughed lightly. "Another parent was supposed to come, but canceled last minute, and I really didn't want to take the boys all alone."

As she spoke, she nibbled her bottom lip. She *was* glad to have a man along, considering her total lack of camping skills. But for some unknown reason Joe Bennett didn't fit the bill. The jeans that hugged his lean hips were perfectly creased and obviously expensive. Why, they actually looked pressed! There was something incongruous—and unsettling—about Joe Bennett.

But there was something even *more* unsettling about taking nine boys to a remote campsite on a rainy autumn evening.

"We're running a little late, Joe. We should get started." Gilly headed for the safety of her car at the same time that Joe began to untie the packed duffels from her luggage rack. She threw him a questioning look.

Joe smiled. "We won't get beyond the city limits in this, ah, vintage automobile." He eyed her rusty Chevy

14

wagon with slight disdain, then nodded toward the van. "Besides, majority rules."

Gilly followed his glance and grimaced as all nine cub scouts waved through open windows, each already settled in the van and ready to go. Her own tousled-haired son Tim stood out from the rest, his look begging her not to ruin things totally by dragging them out of this neat place and back into the clunker.

And beside Tim was Adam, his fair head hanging out the window as he called out over the noise of the others. "Please, Gilly? And I saved you a seat." His voice was so soft Gilly could barely hear the words, but his arms hugged tightly around the empty captain's chair, and the flush of excitement painted across his cheeks was enough.

Gilly Holmes knew when she was licked. She grabbed her backpack and climbed up into the shiny van, pulling the heavy door closed behind her.

The sun was already a brilliant crimson ball sliding down behind the rolling horizon when Gilly, Joe, and the fearless nine reached the Philadelphia city limits and headed north toward Allentown and the Blue Mountains.

Settling back into the soft leather captain's chair Gilly listened to the ceaseless chatter of the cubs.

"This van *is* lovely," she offered presently, opting for light conversation with this very attractive stranger. "It does make traveling with nine rambunctious kids a little easier. Do you use it often?"

"Nope." Joe's eyes left the road for a minute to look at her. "Just got it this afternoon."

Gilly's brows shot up. "What?" Thoughts of muddy boots and grimy hands on virgin upholstery raced across her mind.

"When Adam said we were going camping, I went out and picked it up. This seemed the safest way to travel with a bunch of kids."

Gilly gasped. "Well, maybe! But a motor home would have been nice too—or a chartered plane, or—"

Joe's eyes were now riveted on the highway, and Gilly saw the tension in his grip on the wheel. Obviously this man didn't see the humor in buying a new van for an overnight. Should she mention that she couldn't afford to buy Timmy a new pair of tennis shoes for the trip? No, no, she'd better not. . . .

Swallowing her amazement Gilly focused on refereeing the various comic-book disputes in the rear seats, then settled back and let the scenery fly by in silence.

By the time darkness began wrapping the rolling hills in wonderfully eerie shadows, Joe Bennett was joking familiarly with the kids and his rich, husky laugh seemed as natural in their midst as bubble gum.

Then his dark gaze swung back to Gilly. A faint smile tugged at his lips. "Tell me, Gilly, does being a den mother often take you on camping trips with strange men?"

Gilly let one honied brow climb into her bangs. "Oh, you don't seem so awfully strange, Mr. Bennett."

He watched her bite back a grin and swallowed his own.

"And your husband, what does he think?" Joe was probing for information, and he knew she knew it.

Gilly hesitated, then answered frankly, "I'm not married. My husband died three years ago."

"Oh, I'm sorry," Joe said with genuine remorse. A surprising feeling of guilt washed over him. He hadn't *wanted* there to be a husband, he realized in that instant, but certainly—

"It's all right." Gilly waved aside his discomfort, anxious to change the subject. "Now, Joe, tell me something about you and my friend Adam back there."

"Not much to tell." He smiled, the dimple surfacing against the smooth plane of his cheek. "His mother and I

16

have been divorced for a few years and Adam and I live together in a house with a cook who makes terrible dumplings but loves Adam. She isn't always too terribly fond of me, but is definitely devoted to my son. As is my mother, who visits us from Pittsburgh—often!"

Gilly laughed. "Well, I can see how devoted Adam is to you. He was adamant that you wanted to come along on this camp-out. And look at him; he's talked more this evening than in the six weeks we've had him in the den."

Joe smiled, obviously pleased. "Yes, he was excited to bring the van—and me. I don't think about things like this often enough." He shrugged. "Adam's not a very assertive kid, but he left ten messages with my secretary reminding her to cancel all my appointments today."

"Well, I'm really glad to have you along. I know nothing about camping."

Joe's face fell. "You what? *All* den mothers know about camping. It's genetic!"

"Sorry. I'm a dud in that department, but I follow orders beautifully. Adam has extolled your camping expertise, so we'll be all set."

Joe groaned inwardly at his son's scheming. Adam had seen the full extent of his camping skills: lighting the outdoor barbecue. And it was gas fueled!

A sudden sprinkling of rain drew Joe's strained attention back to the road. He flicked on the wipers. Why had he thought the day had turned sunny? "We're off to a great start: we get to pitch camp in the dark—and in the rain!"

Gilly smiled calmly. "Yes, it looks that way. But the two of us will manage."

The pain between Joe's shoulders knifed its way back with full force. He pressed his lips together and nodded. "Sure," he muttered. "Sure thing!"

Taking a map out of her pocketbook Gilly unfolded it and pointed to a large red *X* some distance above Allen-

17

town. "Here's where we're headed; we're almost there, I should think."

"Great!" Joe squinted through the windshield as the rain kept up a steady patter on the windows. Following Gilly's directions he slowed slightly and pulled onto a two-lane dirt road.

"The parking lot is just a short distance up this road," Gilly offered, "but then there's a short hike up to the campgrounds from there."

"Are you sure?" Suddenly the folds of darkness around them seemed ominous. "Isn't there *some* way we could drive to the site?"

Realization was slowly dawning on Gilly. Her "assistant" was not going to be as helpful as she'd supposed. She sighed deeply and felt the tiredness of the day wrap about her. "That's it, Joe. There's the trail head."

Joe pulled the heavy van into the graveled space and turned off the engine. "Now what?"

Gilly opened the door and the cubs tumbled out of their confinement, laughing, pushing, and filling the damp night air with their shouts.

Gilly hopped out after them. "Okay. *Now* we load our backs with tents and packs, dig the supply of flashlights out of the little green duffel, and grope our way to camp-site number five."

Joe straightened up beside the van, his long, lean form stretching the kinks out of unused muscles. "Where's the green duffel?"

Gilly looked back at the van and waved her hand. "Somewhere in there, I guess. It was in the back of my car."

Joe groaned.

"Oh, no, you didn't! . . . You did?"

"I *didn't* bring it. I *did* bring all the stuff that was piled on top. I thought—"

"Oh, Joe." Gilly moaned. "This is like the blind lead-

18

ing the blind. And all I wanted was *someone* along to *help!*" Gilly brushed away the raindrops clinging to her lashes.

That did him in. Innate chivalry raced through his blood. With sudden, unexpected familiarity he slipped a hand beneath the heavy fall of hair at the nape of her neck and gently massaged away the tension. "Of course I'll help."

The warmth of his sexy, teasing look threw Gilly for a loop. She stepped away.

"Then . . . then let's get organized and hit the trail, fella!"

She grabbed a pair of tents and started to line up the restless scouts. "Do you have a lighter or matches? We're going to need something to light our way."

Joe fished into his jeans pocket and pulled out a small rectangle. "This is all I have."

Gilly took it from his hand with a sigh of relief. When she flicked the switch, a large curl of orange flame brightened the darkness. "This thing's a *torch!*" Her fingers slid over the smooth gold surface, tracing the initials etched into the precious metal.

She watched him for a moment, the flame casting deep shadows across his rugged features, and then he glanced over and caught her staring. One of his surprising, tantalizing smiles lit his face.

"Well, Den Mother, let's not just stand here. Let's go! If these kids are half as hungry as I am, they're going to grab the first squirrel that jumps in their path."

"Right!" Gilly agreed quickly, moving to the head of the line of scouts. "I'll lead with the lighter; you follow to make sure we don't lose anyone."

Joe nodded as he pulled Adam out of the clump of boys and placed him directly in front of himself. Pulling the hood out of Adam's jacket flap he slipped it over his

19

son's damp head. Adam shifted uncomfortably from one foot to the other, then fell quietly back into the line.

The rain had slowed to an almost imperceptible drizzle, but moisture hung thick in the early autumn air. Night sounds whistled from the gnarled shadows of the trees as the bedraggled group made their way slowly down the path.

Breathing in the woodsy odor of rotting branches and leaves, washed clean by the light rain, Gilly groped her way forward, holding the gold lighter out in front of her and praying fervently that there were no bears within a radius of twenty miles.

And from the rear Joe Bennett pushed the boys onward with playful challenges and exaggerated stories of famous frontiersmen. Gilly smiled, liking the sound of his voice and knowing he was there, bringing up the end of her small den like a caboose.

With a careless toss of her head she forged ahead into the darkness.

"Can you go a little faster, Gilly?" Joe yelled over the groans and yawns that were emanating from the small, panting figures between them.

Gilly answered with a quickened pace, stubbing her muddy tennis shoes against fallen branches and thick, twisted roots that jutted menacingly above the ground. She turned to shout back a few words of encouragement. "I think we're almost there, fellas. This part is beginning to look famili—argh!"

There was a squishy thud. Then silence—and darkness.

"Gilly!" Joe's voice shot through the night air. "Gilly, are you all right?"

A muffled sound came back. "Yes, everything's fine but my pride and my jeans. Both are torn to shreds!"

By then Joe was at her side. He disentangled her from the knotted root system that crisscrossed the trail and helped her to her feet. His strong hands smoothed the tangle of wet hair back from her face and then slid down across her shoulders and arms as if to assure himself that she was whole, unbroken. Kneeling down he gently touched the bruised area near her left knee. "Oh, Gilly, I'm sorry!"

Gilly felt the urge to drop into his arms and cry. Instead she tugged her fingers through the damp leaves and twigs caught in her hair and forced a laugh.

"Joe, I'm fine, really. It takes more than a tumble to put me out of commission. But"—she peered through the darkness to see his eyes—"but your lighter. It's down there . . . somewhere." She pointed weakly to the black, shadowed mess of forest debris at their feet. "When I fell, it flew out of my hand."

Convinced Gilly was fine, Joe allowed himself to worry —and get mad. Here they were, trying to find some ridiculous campsite . . . in the dark . . . poorly prepared . . . with nine tired, scraggly kids!

"Any chance you'd like to turn back?" he asked, glaring down at her upturned face. "No—I didn't think so!" Without another word he sank to his knees and began weeding through the leaves at his feet. He came up empty-handed.

"Forget it! We're moving on. Let's go!"

Den Seven shot up like an arrow and drew their soggy packs up over narrow shoulders. Gilly stood silently and watched.

"Joe," she said in a near whisper, wishing she were home in her claw-footed bathtub reading a book of Emily Dickinson's poetry, "Joe, wasn't the lighter valuable?"

Joe's response came without thought. "Valuable? Do you ask a sailor in a storm if the lighthouse is valuable? Sure it is! Without the damn thing we're left out here in the rain, with hungry kids and God knows what else—" He bit off his reply, realizing that nine pairs of scared eyes were staring up at him, hanging on every word. Clearing his throat he added with great bravado, "But what the heck; we're scouts, right, men?"

The boys grinned at the welcome change of tone and nodded in unison. "Right, Mr. Bennett!"

Tim raised his hand, his eyes wide and earnest. "But, Mr. Bennett, if we don't eat pretty soon, we're going to lie right down here and die!"

A chorus of yeahs rounded out Tim's announcement.

Joe grinned at Gilly. "Well, Den Mother, what do *you* think?"

Gilly drew a shaky breath. "Okay, you guys, maybe we'd better call a halt for chow. You all scrunch on down along this path, close together . . . and, Joe, you've got dinner in that blue backpack there."

Joe flipped the pack over one shoulder and loosened the straps as the kids settled back onto the damp ground. His fingers fished through the contents, and soon he pulled out a pack of soggy peanut butter-and-jelly sandwiches, a box of raisins, and can of fruit juice. Holding them close to his eyes to be sure he wasn't feeding them bug spray, Joe tore off the cellophane wrappings and passed his booty around.

"Hey, fellas, this is terrific! Gourmet trail-food!" He glanced over and tried to make out his small son sitting on a giant root. "Adam, they're a little damp, maybe, but still okay, I'm sure—"

Adam shrugged and answered happily, "No problem, Dad. These are great!" His last words were muffled by an enormous bite of mushy peanut butter.

Joe raised one dark brow, then settled back against a massive oak tree. *What the hell am I doing here?* he wondered. It seemed a strange, surrealistic sort of dream. Here he sat with a bedraggled group of wet cub scouts in a blanket of darkness so thick he could feel it; the overhanging trees were gently dripping autumn rain onto his jeans and Windbreaker; and next to him sat an attractive woman who had his pulse strangely racing.

Looking up he traced her outline in the darkness as she sat still on a soggy log, a nubby sweater wrapped around her and her chin cupped in her hands. She had pulled her thick hair back from her face before they began eating, and now raindrops clung to the honey-blond wisps of hair that escaped in front of her ears. She looked at once young and vulnerable, yet tempered by the trials of life—a thin, fine blade made keen by resistance.

His thoughts lingered on her as he chewed on a handful of raisins. Moments later Gilly looked up and caught him still staring. She managed a hint of a smile. "Maybe we'd better move on."

"Yes, ma'am." He saluted smartly, offering a grin and a hand up in the dark.

Between them they managed to arrange the chattering tribe back into order, backpacks in place, and face the narrow trail ahead. "*I'll* lead this time," Joe insisted. "There's just enough moonlight to light my way. Don't worry, we'll be there in no time."

"Of course we will," Gilly added with a burst of confidence. "According to my map it's not much farther."

Gilly's encouraging words lost all meaning after another hour of trudging through the dark forest and forty-seven verses of "A-camping We Will Go!"

"Joe!" she shouted through the night. "Are you *sure* you stayed on the trail? It seemed to fork off a while back, and—"

"I'm sure!" he shouted back. "That was just an animal track. This has to be the way."

I hope, he groaned silently. She was right; there *had* been a fork in the path a while back, but this seemed the more traveled road. What was it that Robert Frost said about the road not taken? Perhaps it was just as well he couldn't remember.

23

Way back in the dark Gilly's concern continued to grow. It was getting on toward midnight, she judged, although her watch had stopped earlier, broken in her fall. Several of the boys appeared to be moving by pure rote, sleepwalking. *Oh, well, maybe they've got the right idea,* she thought, wincing as one of many blisters rubbed against the canvas of her sneaker.

"Hey, gang"—Joe's triumphant call broke the now still night—"we're there! There's a clearing up ahead!"

Disbelief, followed by a rush of pure joy, flooded through Gilly. She raced after the scouts out into a small area of level land where just enough hazy moonlight peeped around clouds to show them each other's weary, dirt-smudged faces, all shining with grinning relief.

"Are you sure this is it?" Gilly whispered, trying to peer through the darkness and find the marker indicating camping site number five.

"Am I sure? Are you crazy? Of course it is!" He dropped his equipment in a heap at his feet. "It's a *beautiful* campsite!"

Gilly ignored him and collected the scouts around her so she could see them. She passed out the tents, answered sleepy questions, and assured the boys there were no bears, wolves, or coyotes in their particular neck of the woods. Then, while the boys busied themselves putting up the small pup tents, she turned her attention to her own tent. And to an empty-handed Joe Bennett, staring at her with a rueful grin.

"Oh, no!" she groaned.

Joe stared at the piece of canvas in her hand. "That's it? For both of us?"

"No, Mr. Bennett." Gilly brushed the back of one hand across her forehead and tried to think. "That's it— for one of us. We'll have to split the boys up; Adam can sleep with you and Timmy can sleep with me."

Shouts of boyish objection were quickly overruled.

24

"That's the way it is, guys," Gilly answered firmly, eyeing all *three* males with a look that brooked no argument.

Gilly slipped into her tent. A little while later Joe was back again. "Just wanted to report in that everyone is sleeping, Den Mother."

"Not *everyone.*" She stuck her head out through the tent flap and eyed him cautiously. "Why don't you get to bed?" Her whisper played on the night air, drawing him closer.

He knelt down beside her, watching her in the darkness until Gilly squirmed with discomfort.

"Go to bed!"

"Not yet. Too much on my mind." Without warning Joe reached out and stroked the back of his fingers down the curve of her cheek.

Gilly felt her blood race. "What was that for?"

"I just couldn't stop myself. I've been wanting to touch you all evening." There was the briefest pause, and then his husky voice continued, "Why? Did it bother you?"

"Not really."

Gilly assured herself that it was *not* his nearness, but rather the strong, musky odor of rich earth and autumn foliage that was making her head spin. She ducked farther into the shadows of the tent. "Go away! I've got enough sense to go to sleep—even if you don't!"

As he walked away, she thought she heard Joe Bennett laugh. Low and rich, it was a laugh that held a hint of amusement and a hint of promise.

Quick as a wink Gilly slid into her sleeping bag and squinched her eyelids tightly together, barely feeling the hard earth beneath her. What was happening to her? What had happened to this whole crazy day? And who in heaven's name was Joe Bennett?

Warmth and exhaustion soon slowed her thoughts.

But sleep was a long time coming. All Gilly's senses were fully awake, her thoughts playing with the image of

Joe, so close outside the tent. And then she heard the sudden rhythmic ping of raindrops on canvas. She grinned wickedly. *That* would get him to bed.

The rain had done its job well, ushering in a soft, mist-shrouded dawn that blanketed the woods in warm golden hues. Gilly emerged from the tent to the welcoming chorus of crickets and birds shaking dewdrops from their feathers.

Stretching, she breathed in the crisp, clean air, then automatically checked the tiny tents and accounted for all the occupants. *And* Joe, who was exactly where she had expected him to be, his long legs protruding from beneath the uneven edge of Adam's tent. She bit back her laughter.

Finally her eyes scanned a larger circle and took in the surrounding area.

For a moment she stood frozen, as if she had awakened in the middle of a dream and hadn't yet settled back into reality. And then Gilly Holmes lost her cool. Wrapping her arms around herself she doubled over, convulsed in laughter. She covered her mouth to muffle the sound as the tears began to stream down her face. Leaning against a tree she laughed and laughed.

As the cub scouts tumbled out of their tents, one by one, Gilly fed them doughnuts and orange juice dug from the depths of the packs, bribing them into silence.

Finally, when the sun had shed its haze and traveled to treetop height, Joe Bennett stirred in his tent. He turned over and felt the uneven space beside him, but his son was gone. Opening his eyes he saw the light and the bright bars of morning sun outlining the small door-flap. He smiled, pleased and proud of himself. He'd gotten them to the campsite; they'd somehow managed to pitch camp in the darkness in the middle of the woods, and

26

they'd all had a decent night's sleep. Sometimes things *did* work out after all!

A soft buzz beyond the tent caught his attention. The boys must be up, must be out there with Gilly. The buzz sounded like muffled laughter, and curiosity got the best of him. Yawning, Joe Bennett stretched, unfolded his stiff body, and emerged into a pool of sunlight.

He saw Gilly first, her gleeful smile erupting into a shout of laughter; the cubs surrounded her, their faces smeared with jelly doughnuts, their giggles popping like tiny firecrackers.

Then he looked around their campsite; he looked forward and backward, his dark eyes roving across the wide, clean-swept area, his own lips curving in a rueful smile. For everywhere he looked he met the welcoming, curious glances of residents of the Oakpark Trailer Camp, sitting on the very civilized porches of their modern trailers enjoying a cup of morning coffee. The gravel parking lot, with the top of the shiny new van just visible through the branches of the trees, lay just beyond.

CHAPTER TWO

"Hey, where's the press type for these comps? I've got to get them to the client tonight, Gilly. Gilly? You with me? Gillian, what do ya say, pardner?"

"What? Oh, sorry, Tugg, did you say something?"

"Not much. Just revamped the entire project, changed the company name. Small things like that." A broad wink flashed above a tangle of beard. "You were so quiet I thought you were either deep in aesthetic contemplation of our packaging design—or dead."

"Definitely the former," Gilly joked back, feeling the blood rush to her face. She'd been caught, and she knew it. Her blush deepened.

"Or," Tugg Waters continued undaunted, "is there perchance a third possibility? Such as 'I left my heart in a Blue Mountain campsite . . .'?" Tugg's Nikon camera swung from a thick strap around his neck as he swayed from side to side doing the world's worst Tony Bennett imitation.

Gilly slapped at him with a rolled layout sheet. "Cut that out, Tugg!"

"Sure, kiddo, sure." Her partner in the fledgling graphic arts firm of Holmes and Waters readily acquiesced. He was glad to see that sparkle of excitement in her eyes.

Gilly was sorry she had ever mentioned a word about her crazy weekend. Maybe *talking* about it was the reason she didn't seem to be able to erase Joe Bennett from her thoughts. Talking about it and the odd, anxious sensation that had plagued her all week long.

Scowling, she tapped a finger impatiently on the drawing board. "Now, back to this design." Leaning her chin on the clasped backs of her hands, she scrutinized the layout. "You know, I think we ought to stick with the blue background for the pineapples. It's neat and classy. If I redo this rendering here and enlarge the lettering a bit . . ."

Kicking off her moccasins she tucked her feet up beneath her. In her powder-blue warm-up suit, her thick hair tied back in a ponytail, Gilly looked younger than twenty-nine, like a kid again almost, untouched by the problems of the past few years.

Tugg watched her for a moment from behind a batch of negatives hanging over his desk, then walked over and looked at her layout. "Looks good, kid. Hey, I've been thinking. I like to see you look the way you do today, kinda peaceful. But it's an oddity these days."

Gilly's brows lifted in puzzlement.

"What I mean is, that hostessing job at the restaurant—"

"No, Tugg. I won't give it up. It's only part-time, and besides the fact that it's paying for our enlarger, it's kind of a nice break."

"But maybe it's my turn to work a couple extra jobs—"

29

"Tugg!" Gilly laughed. "How many more kids' birthday-party pictures and weddings can you take on before you disappear in a cake? You're doing more than your share."

Tugg walked back to his desk. "I just don't want you to get too swallowed up in work, Gilly."

"Okay, Tugg, I promise. Now, stop worrying about the world and let's get this layout figured out! Timmy'll be home—"

"Mom—I'm starving!" The back door slammed shut and Tim burst into the dining-room-turned-studio, brown hair falling over his eyebrows.

"No hellos?"

"Oops. Sorry. Hi, Mom. Hey, Tugg, what's doing, man? Mom, I'm starved."

Gilly smiled, ruffled Tim's hair, and made a mental note to fit in a trip to the barber. "Okay. Fix yourself a snack and we'll think about dinner later. How was soccer practice?"

"It was great! Like *what* for dinner?"

"Like I don't know. Grab an apple for now, Timmy, and—"

"Oh, Mom." Tim groaned. "That means salad and tuna fish again!"

"Fish is good—"

"—for your brain. I know! I've probably got the strongest brain in third grade. Another can of tuna and I'm gonna turn into a genius! Can't we go to McDonald's?" He shoved his hands in the pockets of worn jeans and gave Gilly a pleading look.

"Nope." Gilly laughed, shaking her head firmly. "We're out of 'eat-out' funds until next month. Here, first tell me what you think about this new layout, and then take Henry out for a walk; he's been waiting at the gate for you all afternoon. He seems to sense when it's Friday and the boys will all be coming—oh, my Lord!" Gilly

30

slapped a hand across her mouth and flew off the chair, scattering pencils and papers onto the floor.

Henry barked at the unexpected excitement just as the doorbell rang.

"The cubs! It's Friday, Timmy! Why didn't you remind me?"

"You knew it was Friday when I left for school this morning, Mom. *You* reminded me! Sounds like you need the tuna more than I do." Timmy chuckled at his own joke and took a playful kung-fu lunge at Tugg.

Gilly groaned and stared at the clock.

Outside, Joe Bennett stood on the porch, wondering what in the world he was doing there. Damn, he had a million things on his mind, a pile of work higher than Adam sitting on his desk at home, *and* the third visit from his mother in less than six weeks.

He glanced down at his three-piece suit. Not exactly what assistant den-leaders wore, but it was the best he could handle on a schedule that barely allowed time for eating, much less changing clothes.

The damn camp-out had been eating away at the edges of his thoughts all week. He'd find himself smiling at odd moments as he pictured those crazy hours. And crazy is exactly what they were. Certainly not something he'd invest any more time in, except that Adam, bless his youthful soul, announced that Joe was the assistant for the month. *All* the mothers took a turn, after all! And that tone was all Joe needed to assure Adam he'd be there, in body, if not in spirit.

Forking his fingers through his dark hair he peered at the stained-glass window set high in the front door. It was much too high for Gilly Holmes to see out. No, she'd come just about here, he thought, to the angle of his shoulder, her thick red-gold hair brushing his chin. An unexpected smile broke across his face, easing the finely

31

etched lines across his forehead, and he pressed his finger into the doorbell again.

Inside, Gilly quickly scooped up scattered layout sheets as Tim raced through the hall and skidded to a stop at the door. He flung it open, then stared at the man looking down at him. As Henry barked in greeting, Timmy grinned. "Hi."

"Hello. Is your mother home?"

"Yeah, sure. Wait a minute, okay?" Tim started to turn, then wheeled back to the door and subjected the caller to another head-to-toe scrutiny. His eyes flew wide. "Hey, it's you, isn't it? Adam's dad! I didn't recognize you without your backpack!"

"I'm travelin' light." Joe grinned, then prompted, "Your mother's here, right? It's Friday."

"Oh, sure. Yeah, she's here." Pivoting on one sneaker Tim yelled through the house, "Hey, Mom, it's our camp-out assistant!"

"What?" The pencil Gilly was holding clattered to the floor. She turned sharply and headed for the door, hopping on one foot when the other gave way to a rush of pins-and-needles. She caught the door frame to steady herself and looked up at Joe.

"Hi!"

"Hi." Joe's dark eyes clouded at her limp. "You're not hurt from that tumble you took on the trail, are you?"

Gilly laughed away his words, uncomfortable with such solicitations. "Oh, no, I'm too tough for that. My foot fell asleep while I was working, that's all. How are you? All recovered?"

She clasped both hands tightly behind her back and looked up at him from beneath those straight, heavy bangs. It made his heart jump. Her eyes were so blue, cornflower-blue, and suddenly Joe found himself thinking of flowers and meadows and the lovely way she had smiled as she stood beside the scouts.

Gilly felt herself melt beneath the unexpected heat of his look. Her heart was pounding like a bass drum in her throat and it took an effort to squeak the words out. "Please, Joe—come in."

"Sure. Thanks."

He followed her into the house thinking how damned adorable she was in her warm-ups, and noticing the light, athletic grace of her walk, the bounce to her step. Even the fact that she was barefooted pleased him for some unknown reason.

But when she turned and caught him looking, he shifted his eyes quickly to the room they had entered. There were handsome photographic prints on the dining-room wall, a bare minimum of furniture, and a clutter of press type, enlargers, reams of paper, and jars of pencils on the tabletops. But what held Joe's eyes longest was the bearded stranger leaning against one of the cabinets with a casualness that suggested he somehow belonged there.

"Joe Bennett"—the sound of his name on her lips brought his attention back to Gilly—"I'd like you to meet Tugg Waters, my business partner. Tugg, meet Joe Bennett."

Tugg grinned, shaking hands enthusiastically. "Ah, the fearless guide, tracker, and modern-day Daniel Boone."

Joe tried halfheartedly to match the man's enthusiasm. "One and the same. But you've got an edge up on me, Tugg. I didn't know Gilly had a business partner, let alone a business!"

"Oh? Well, what did you two talk about all night in that godforsaken campsite?"

"Camping!" Gilly said, shushing him.

Joe laughed shortly, pinning Gilly with watchful eyes. "I've managed to block much of that night from memory, but I know you never mentioned this. Here I've been picturing a starving artist in her lonely garret."

"For sure starving!" Tim piped up from his forgotten

33

corner of the room, then quickly dodged his mother's look and headed toward the kitchen with Tugg in tow.

"Well," Gilly answered, "hopefully *those* days are nearly past." Knocking on wood for superstition's sake Gilly shifted the conversation back to Joe. "Where's Adam?"

"He'll be dropped off. I came right from work—"

Gilly's brows drew into a confused look.

"—to help. Adam says I'm to help out this week."

There was just the slightest note of irritation in his eyes.

Gilly took a quick gulp of air, then nodded enthusiastically. "Of course! I'm sorry, but I'm not always clear on who's coming when." She ruffled through some papers curled into a wicker basket near her layout table and spotted Joe's name printed in Adam's unmistakable scribble on the parent volunteer sheet. She'd have to be more careful to check the assistants ahead of time, she resolved silently. Surprises like this she could do without!

"It was nice of you to offer to help like this, Joe. I'm sure it's not easy finding time." She laughed lightly and waved the air with the papers. "Goodness knows, I have a hard time doing it!"

"Yes. But if my deductions from dinner-table talk are correct, you've been a huge success. Adam talks about you in the same breath with his new dirt bike. And with equal enthusiasm." The compliment was unexpected and carried on a deep, husky tone that made Gilly shift and concentrate on finding her moccasins beneath the drawing table.

Sunlight dappled the small patch of floor around her bare feet, liquid and golden as puddles of sweet cream.

Joe's gaze settled into the warming color. For a brief moment, as he stood there quietly with Gilly Holmes at his side, he felt some of the day's tension ease away. Then he blinked, looked at the floor more clearly, then up at Gilly. "Your floor is yellow. I mean, it's all yellow!"

"I know." She lifted one shoulder disarmingly. "It was the first thing I did when I bought this little house. Pulled out the carpeting and painted it myself. I knew the sunlight would dance here in the afternoons."

"How did you know?" he asked. At that moment he only wanted her to go on talking for a long time, semiserious, intent, and charming.

Gilly looked at the curve of his mouth, his broad cheekbones, the umber depths of his eyes, and she liked what she saw. It took her breath away.

Quickly she tried to dispel it with a toss of her gold-flecked hair.

"Yes, well, Joe, now that you're here, I'm sure you're wondering what's on the agenda today." Gilly quickly ran over the scribbled words on the top sheet of paper, then looked up from beneath the fringe of thick lashes. "I really am more organized about all this than my studio might suggest. Here—look." She thrust the paper in front of him and smiled. "See? Almost the whole year outlined for Den Seven. Well, there're a few gaps maybe, but that allows us to be spontaneous now and then."

"And today? What's it to be, programed or spontaneous?"

"Oh, programed, definitely. *Very* programed." She stretched out the *very* in a way that drew Joe's smile back to the surface.

"Oh?"

"Yes, as a matter of fact, today is Skinner day."

"As in—"

Gilly pointed a pencil at him. "Right on, Mr. Bennett. B.F. himself. The boys are doing their own thought-up science project. It's quite creative for eight-year-olds."

"And the subjects are?"

Thuds, scrapes, and what sounded briefly like a million

high-pitched voices coming from the back door blurred Gilly's answer and she and Joe headed toward the noise now coming from the kitchen. Obviously the scouts had arrived, but that didn't account for the screeching noises.

Gilly muffled a laugh behind one hand as she stood in the doorway surveying the scene.

Every inch of space, what little there was, was now crammed full of wire cages containing crying, screeching guinea pigs.

"Real guinea pigs . . ." Joe murmured.

Gilly laughed. "Certainly, real guinea pigs. Stuffed animals aren't much good in mazes. These boys are serious about this."

"Hi, Dad. See mine?" Adam held up a black-and-white critter and the youngster's eyes shone brightly. "Davey loaned me one of his because I don't have one and his keep havin' babies. See? He brought 'em all along."

Joe stared at the tiny wriggling forms in the straw-strewn cage and turned toward Gilly. "They don't . . . uh, carry diseases or bugs, do they?"

Gilly hid her surprise by bending over a cage and fastening the latch. Didn't all little boys have guinea pigs or hamsters or a hermit crab or two? Obviously not Adam Bennett, although in Gilly's opinion he probably needed a soft creature to pet more than most of her cubs. Oh, well, it really wasn't her business. She stood up straight. "No, Joe, I don't think so. A flea or two, perhaps, but then, it's all in the name of science." She smiled brightly, greeted the boys enthusiastically, and began giving directions as to where to put their cages.

Tugg pulled his head out of the refrigerator long enough to suggest building the maze in the basement, then quickly resumed his search for sustenance.

Joe watched him for a moment, then directed his attention back to the scouts. Their small, energetic bodies were in constant movement, rivaled only by that of the squirming colony of guinea pigs stacked up near the kitchen table. He made an instant decision.

"Gilly." Joe tapped her on the shoulder as she gently soothed the curly-haired owner of a pinched finger.

"Yes?" Her hair swung past his face in a clean-smelling breeze as she turned to face him.

"We'll move the meeting to my house. There's more room." He bent over and picked up one of the cages. "It'll be safer, more efficient. . . ."

Gilly stared after him as he moved toward the door. "Stop, Joe"—her hand flew after him, just clipping the edge of his shoulder—"wait. What do you mean, 'move to your house'?" The tilt of several towheads made her realize her voice was rising and she quickly nudged Joe back into the studio, lowering her voice to a fierce hush. "Mr. Bennett, the meetings are always held here, and it's always worked out just fine. We've had obstacle courses with gerbils, dress-up-your-dog day—lots of things! And there's always been plenty of room!" Her forehead drew into a tight frown as she clamped her fists on her narrow hips and bent slightly forward from the waist. "And what in heaven's name is unsafe about my home?"

Joe watched in surprise the flash of anger in her lovely blue stare. "Gilly, no offense was intended. But you have to admit, this isn't exactly an ideal spot for nine cub scouts and this . . . this multitude of fur. I was merely suggesting a practical, sensible solution. We have a large recreation room in the basement which would be ideal for the boys' experiment. It makes much more sense."

Gilly nibbled on her bottom lip, trying to blot out flashing visions of guinea pigs getting stuck forever behind her washing machine, or buried beneath stacks of boxes piled in her cobwebby basement. He was right, of course. She didn't have the ideal place. But it was the principle of the thing. It was Joe Bennett's instinctive urge to step in and take over that bothered Gilly. She'd seen it on the camp-out, and now he was doing it again, and in that same smooth, suave, used-to-getting-his-own-way manner. She'd become quite adept these past few years at resisting such techniques, but dealing with a man who left her breathless and vaguely lightheaded was another matter.

"Gilly"—it was Tugg speaking now from the doorway, his beard dotted with telltale crumbs of pie crust—"if you do use the basement, try not to mess up the negatives hanging across the middle of the room, okay? They're like gold, ya know?" And he winked, causing Gilly's frown to deepen and a defeated groan to escape her lips.

It seemed like a conspiracy, but perhaps she was simply tired. That must be it. She forced a smile at her silly irritation against a man she scarcely knew, who was merely trying to help run a scout meeting. Her brows lifted slowly as her hands fell to her sides.

"Your car or mine?" she asked with a slow grin. Then, without waiting for an answer, she moved to the kitchen to collect stray scouts and guinea pigs and pack them in the shiny van she knew would be waiting outside the front door.

The road led quickly away from the old comfortable Germantown neighborhood and onto the hectic freeway.

As he guided the van through the traffic with one hand, Joe rested his arm along the window ledge and took a quick glance at Gilly. When the wind swept through her hair, it spilled across her shoulder like honey. Her cheeks were flushed from the cool breeze and her eyes sparkled as they moved along the passing terrain. He shook his head and tried to clear his mind.

"So, Gilly Holmes, you're a businesswoman. Tell me about your partner." His voice was low and controlled, and Gilly answered readily.

"Yes, well, Tugg is unique. He's very clever, very talented. We met in art school and became good friends, and when we completed the program last June, we decided we'd go on working together. That was the beginning of Holmes and Waters. It's been an uphill struggle, but things get a little better each month. And it has been wonderful not having to climb all the rough spots alone." Gilly's light laughter filled Joe's head.

"Is there anyone else?"

"No, just the two of us."

"No, I mean is there anyone else I need to know about?"

Gilly stared at him. Had she heard him right? The abrupt personal question was asked with the ease of discussing the weather! What business was it of Joe Bennett's whether or not there was a man in her life? She bit back the retort and quickly shifted her gaze to the passing countryside.

"Well?" he prompted gently.

Well? Well, what, Gilly Holmes? And why in heaven's name aren't you telling him to back off? "Well, if you mean Tugg—"

"I mean anyone. Including Tugg."

His calmness unnerved Gilly, and she tried to dispel it with a light laugh. "Tugg and I are very good friends, but his taste in women runs along more avant-garde lines; his most recent girlfriend had purple hair! Besides"—she shifted in the seat, feeling a welcome wave of confidence return—"I have a very busy life, with Tim and the business, and PTA, and—"

"*And* playing den mother to nine little Indians!"

"Right."

"Wrong. There should be time for you in there somewhere."

Incredulous laughter spilled out of her. "Joe Bennett, that *is* time for me—Tim and my business—they're a part of me. It's just that I've set a few priorities, and they're all I have time for. Now, may we change the subject or would you rather we set up our maze in that field over there?"

"Difficult, aren't you?"

"Definitely! Take it or leave it."

Joe took it, with a strange, almost foreign feeling of delight. He fell silent, resting his arm back on the window ledge and watching the road fly by.

"Where are we going?" Gilly asked a few moments later, glancing at the sign they passed as they turned off the highway.

"I told you, my place."

One look at the rolling lawns and manicured hedges told Gilly exactly where they were. Philadelphia's Main Line, an area of lavish homes and great wealth.

"Oh, no, Joe," she groaned as he pulled to a sharp stop at the entrance to a long, curving drive. A row of elm trees and a high stone fence shielded the house beyond from the noise and traffic of the road. Joe pressed a hidden button above his visor and the gates swung open.

"Oh, no, what?"

"Oh, no, as in 'this isn't the kind of house to experiment with guinea pigs in'!"

"Don't be silly. It's just home," he answered, pulling his attention away from her startled gaze and focusing on the house ahead.

Gilly followed his glance. It was an old home built of rough-cut stone with a wide-arched doorway and lovely tall windows. An architect's dream and an artist's delight. Her imagination slipped inside, envisioning cushioned window seats and high ceilings trimmed with finely carved woodwork, wide hallways, and spacious rooms. And even a grand staircase leading to the upper level.

She wasn't disappointed. When Joe opened the door and stepped aside to let the cubs tear through, then calmly motioned for Gilly to follow, she felt the house breathe a welcome. The boys and cages disappeared immediately and Gilly stood quietly taking it all in.

A light breeze wafting through the open door of the parlor carried the faint tick-tock of a grandfather clock. Curtains rustled somewhere in an unseen room and music wafted in from a stereo in the distance. The muted sounds blended, floating up to the vaulted ceilings that made Gilly feel small and hushed.

"Joe, this is a lovely home. A lovely, happy home . . ."

"Happy enough," he stated flatly. His eyes dared her to question him.

Tilting her chin up Gilly retorted, "And what does that mean?"

"Just what I said." There was a slight, controlled smile beneath the words, but Gilly found it difficult to interpret.

"Well, I for one never could understand how happy 'happy enough' is. That's like being 'a little bit pregnant.' You're either happy or you're not!"

Joe looked at Gilly curiously for a moment. Then, without pursuing the subject, he touched her arm gently and guided her into the next room.

"This is beautiful!" Gilly's eyes gleamed in appreciation of the old hardwood floors and pieces of antique furniture.

"Glad you approve." He moved past her, letting his arm brush lightly against her shoulder as he entered the library.

Gilly shivered unexpectedly, then shifted her attention quickly to the beautiful, imposing room. Her lively imagination could invent a fire crackling in the yawning brick fireplace, but now there was not even a trace of ash. In the floor-to-ceiling bookcases the books stood side by side, each precisely in line with the one before and the one after. The leather couch looked soft and warm as cinnamon toast, but there was no comfortable indentation where a head had rested, or someone had curled up with legs tucked up beneath an afghan on a cool fall evening. No casual pillow. No open magazine or half-read book. No pipe waiting in a nearby ashtray.

Her own tiny living room leapt to mind. The sunny yellow floor, her off-white, slightly worn couch that was a bit lopsided from where Tugg had knocked off a caster when they moved it in. A couple of easy chairs her neighbor had covered in bright prints set cozily in front of the small television, and Timmy's fielder's glove, books, and endless collection of baseball cards shoved into all available space.

Suddenly she felt like an intruder here in this elegant room, a tourist on a walk through some empty, echoing museum where people used to live, who wanders away from her tour group and finds herself behind the ribboned walkway. Careful not to touch she hurried after Joe and found him in the kitchen.

He was standing near the phone, jotting notes on a small pad as he listened intently to the voice at the other end.

Feeling her presence Joe turned and smiled. In seconds he hung up the phone. A fine webbing of lines crinkled around his dark eyes. "Did you think I deserted you? Sorry. I got waylaid by a business call and—"

"Listen, take your time. I know how that can be, business and all."

"No, it will wait," he insisted. It would wait; the whole world would wait if it had to. "Now, what was I—oh, the scouts. Yes, mazes . . ."

Gilly laughed huskily. "Yes, Joe. The scouts. Skinner, remember?"

"Of course. I thought I'd grab a bag of ice and we can give them a cold drink before we start."

Gilly nodded, surprised. She hadn't expected Joe Bennett to think of such things—ordinary needs like hunger and thirst. Her surprise was cut short as Joe opened the freezer door.

She felt the cold breeze, then heard the bumps, and saw the bouncing parade of frozen chickens scooting across the shiny kitchen floor.

Gilly's mouth flew open.

Joe stared.

It was an avalanche of chickens, each one frozen separately in clear plastic wrap.

Joe's shout of laughter surprised Gilly, catching her up in its spell. She dropped to her knees next to him to retrieve the wayward pullets.

"My mother!" He grinned.

"Really? Mine collected teacups."

With another burst of husky laughter Joe rocked back on his heels. "Well, I wouldn't quite call this 'collecting.' It's more of a charm to ward off evil spirits."

Gilly contemplated him from beneath the fringe of her bangs. Was he putting her on? But there was a revealing openness in his compelling dark eyes.

"Well, I think it definitely works. I haven't seen an evil spirit since I arrived."

"I think that's your magic more than hers." He smiled.

His shoulder touched hers, his breath feathering her cheek.

Gilly tilted her head to see into his eyes, and then his arms went around her. Pulling her close against him Joe kissed her full on the mouth.

"What are you doing?" she murmured.

"Well," he murmured, brushing his lips lightly across hers, "I think I'm kissing you . . . an ancient custom I'm actually quite fond of."

"But *why,* Mr. Bennett?"

"Because there's nothing I'd rather be doing in the

whole world," he answered in a husky whisper against her mouth.

And since Gilly couldn't think of a single thing she'd rather do, she kissed him back, soft and fully, and not at all feeling like a den mother with nine scouts loose in the basement of this wonderful man's home.

"Ahem." It was a soft, kind "ahem," and registered gently in Gilly's consciousness, melding together with the wonderful warmth of Joe's body.

"The chickens . . ." the silvery voice continued. "Shall I help you pick them up before they fly away?"

Gilly pulled herself away, feeling an uncomfortable rush of cold saneness return. Still on her knees she looked beyond Joe's broad shoulder to a shadow in the doorway, a small white-haired shadow with twinkling eyes and an ample bosom covered by an old-fashioned bibbed apron.

"Joseph"—the figure took a step toward them and her smile widened—"I don't believe I've met your friend." Warm brown eyes twinkled merrily in the woman's softly lined face.

Joe quickly stood and pulled Gilly to her feet. He shook his head in amusement as he took Gilly's arm. "Gilly Holmes, I'd like you to meet the owner of this flock—Mary Bennett, my mother."

CHAPTER THREE

Gilly should have been embarrassed, she reflected later, but Mary Bennett absolutely forbade it. In a sweeping movement that was as warm and comforting as Joe's kiss had been sensual, she ushered Gilly over to the round oak kitchen table.

"So at last I meet Gilly, Adam's beloved den mother." Hundreds of tiny lines fanned out from her eyes as she looked warmly at Gilly and patted her hand. "What a delight!"

"Yes, Mother," Joe interrupted, shoving the last of the chickens back into the freezer. "And she's here in an official capacity. Adam's den is downstairs, preparing an experiment—"

"Yes, dear, I know," Mary Bennett answered her son patiently. "Den Seven and I have become fast friends. That little Timmy is a caution." She smiled at Gilly. "But they have made one slight mistake in their experiment."

Gilly's brows shot up.

"Now, dear, don't fret. But I do need a few more hands to collect the creatures. You see, the little boys didn't order their activities exactly right. They let the guinea pigs out of the cages *before* they built the mazes. . . ."

Gilly was out of the room before she realized she had no idea where the basement stairs were. The sole thought hammering wildly in her head was that there were over two dozen guinea pigs loose in Joe's basement!

Joe was behind her in seconds, guiding her toward a wide back hallway that led to a set of carpeted stairs. And from then on the noise of giggling, shrieking eight-year-olds took over and there was no doubt where the guinea pigs were romping.

They scampered beneath the lovely upholstered couch; they cowered behind the bar; they scrambled under the game table and television set. The tiny babies, less afraid than their adult counterparts, ran in merry circles atop the pool table, tumbling happily into the pockets. And nine little blue-shirted scouts scampered after them, having the time of their lives.

Gilly tore her eyes away from the bedlam for a moment and sought out Joe. She found him in a corner, a serious frown running across his forehead as he systematically scooped up and deposited the squirming animals into random cages. He still had his suit coat on and Gilly suppressed a grin at the incongruous portrait he made, his tie dipping with each bend, his brows nearly touching one another as he concentrated on the distasteful task before him.

"He's too serious, my Joseph." Mary stood quietly beside her, watching the methodical movements. "He needs to taste more of life." The elderly woman patted Gilly's arm gently and sought out her eyes. "And you, Gilly? Tell me about you."

Gilly bit back a smile. Here they stood in the middle of

utter chaos, and Mary Bennett was as calm as a saint and wanted to have a talk. Gilly turned toward her warmly.

"Right now my life is Timmy. And a small business I've started with a friend."

She spoke the words proudly, and Mary nodded, pleased.

"And you manage?"

"Yes, quite nicely." Gilly smiled and ran one hand through her thick hair. "Oh, it's not always easy. Timmy sometimes needs me one hundred and fifty percent of the time, and the business another hundred percent, and . . ." Her voice died off as she watched Joe tackle a guinea pig.

Mary laughed with kind understanding. "And that leaves minus time for Gilly's spirit. But I can see you manage beautifully, dear. That sparkle in your eye is a dead giveaway." She waved her hand in the air. "Hard times, difficult times, they go away eventually . . . and you forget." Her gaze lingered on Joe, and for a brief second Gilly caught a sadness in her eyes. But it disappeared in an instant when her small grandson dashed up to her excitedly.

"Gram, isn't this the greatest?" After shoving a black-and-white guinea pig into her hands he disappeared in a flash.

"Adam is such a dear boy." Mary petted the animal absently as her crinkling eyes followed the energetic body lovingly across the room.

"Your only grandchild?" Gilly asked.

"Yes. Joe's brother isn't married." She hesitated for just a brief moment. "And Adam is Joe's only child. . . ."

"Well, you have a fine grandson, Mary," Gilly said warmly.

Mary's response was lost in a deep groan from the corner of the room. Gilly glanced over to see Joe stiffly unbending his long frame from the floor. His jaw was clenched, his brows a thundercloud over dark flashing eyes.

Gilly looked at Mary, but she had moved away and was busy ushering the scouts around the corner to the bar area for sodas.

The faint sound of cursing drew Gilly's attention back to the dim corner. Slowly she stepped around filled guinea-pig cages and approached Joe.

"What's the matter?"

"Starting from the top of the list?" His voice was low and irritated.

"No. Let's just have the latest. Whatever it was that's making you look pained and miserable. And remember when you answer, that coming here was *your* idea."

Joe glared at her, then stiffly shifted his body so his suit coat pulled away from his side. "It's one of those damn guinea pigs. The little ones—"

Gilly's brows shot up, and she scanned his face for explanation. Finding none, she looked down at his awkward pose. This time she saw it clearly—a slowly moving lump, purposefully clawing its way around Joe Bennett's waist!

Gilly's hand shot to her mouth as her eyes widened. "Oh . . . Joe. What's he doing in there?" Her voice fluctuated as she tried to dispel the giggles erupting wildly in her throat.

"I haven't had a chance to ask," Joe hissed. "Now, would you kindly get it out?"

"Me?" Gilly took a step back.

"I can't reach it, Gilly, damn it!" He strained to see the lump that was now in the center of his back.

"Just kneel down and pull your shirt out. He'll drop. Hopefully."

"He's attached. To me! Get him—" Joe stopped, took a deep steadying breath, and went on more amicably.

48

"Please, just get him out. Now, Gilly. Out of my shirt, my house, my life." He tried to muster a humorous tone as he let his suit jacket slip down his arms and onto the floor.

Gilly moved around behind Joe and pulled his starched shirt out of the waistband of his pants. As she slipped her hand up his back, the giggles dissolved in her throat. She tried desperately to fill her mind with images of guinea pigs—funny, furry little creatures—but all that came forth were tantalizing visions of the smooth, heated body her hand was slowly canvassing.

Stop it, Gillian Marie Holmes, she scolded fiercely. *You're not supposed to be enjoying this!* But try as she might, the hot, tingling sensations that surged through her tense body grew stronger. Finally, with great effort, she wrapped her fingers around the tiny, frightened guinea pig now firmly attached to Joe's undershirt, and gently began to tug him free.

"Oww!" Joe yelped.

"Sorry, Joe," Gilly mumbled, grateful he couldn't see the deep, hot flush that spread across her face. "He seems to be attached."

"I'm well aware of that. The damnable creature needs a manicure!"

Gilly swallowed hard. She had no choice. Holding the guinea pig firmly in one hand she slipped her free hand beneath the T-shirt, up the firm, muscular surface of Joe's back, and pried the tiny claws from his skin. It took a fraction of a second—and lasted a lifetime. Joe's skin was warm and slightly damp, the sheen of perspiration a layer of stretched silk beneath her fingertips. She felt the roll of muscles as he strained his shoulders, then tightly closed her eyes to dispel the vivid sensations that each slight movement precipitated. But the darkness only heightened the wonderful feel of him, and Gilly fought the nearly overwhelming urge to press her fingers into his flesh.

Lord, she thought, *what's happening to me? I'm acting as if I've never touched a man before!* She pulled her hands from beneath his shirt as if they'd suddenly hit hot coals, then carefully dropped the animal in the nearest cage.

She wanted to hide. Her pulse was racing and tiny beads of perspiration appeared from nowhere on her brow. The temptation to return to the smooth, wonderful feel of Joe Bennett began to ease at last and she released a long, slow breath.

"Well?"

"Well, what?" Gilly mumbled from her bent position over the wire cage.

"Well, are you going to climb into the cage or come up here where I can thank you?" There was a slight trace of amusement in Joe's sexy voice.

"No need for thanks," she murmured as she raised herself up, busily scanning the room for any other stray guinea pigs. "Plucking guinea pigs off backs is all in the line of duty." She forced a smile and met his eyes. They seemed to have deepened three shades since she had last looked.

As she took a step backward, Gilly shook her head to clear the air. There, that felt much better. Things were falling back into focus. She was competent, energetic Gilly Holmes again, den leader, graphic artist, mother of Tim. And Joe Bennett was nothing more than the slightly scratched father of one of her cubs.

"Now, Joe, let's put those pigs through their paces before they're too old to hobble, shall we?"

And she led him quickly out of the shadows, around the corner, and into the safe, noisy fray of scouts.

* * *

"Well, it wasn't necessary, you know." Gilly rested her head back against the cool leather of Joe's foreign sports car, which he had chosen to drive instead of the large van. "Insisting we all eat, then inviting the whole den to stay over. Those boys are going to wear your mother out."

"You don't know Mary Bennett, Gilly. She loves being around children—says it's what keeps her young." His voice grew thoughtful as he steered the small car eastward. "In fact, she spends a good part of each visit urging me to have Adam invite friends over, but somehow we seldom get around to it. I don't know, maybe my mother's right. Adam did seem excited at the idea of having the boys stay to watch a movie in the little theater."

"Of course he was. But not nearly as thrilled as the boys were! Tim couldn't get over the idea of someone having a movie theater in his own home." Gilly took a quick glance sideways at Joe's intent profile. "It *is* a bit unusual, Joe. Do you entertain a lot? In the theater, I mean?" She knew she was treading on waters that might best be left still—Joe Bennett's whole manner warned against talk of his personal life—but Gilly was frankly curious.

"No, I don't entertain often at home." His voice was clipped, slightly formal.

"The theater, then—?"

"It was a present for Adam."

"Oh." An eight-year-old with his own theater. Gilly felt suddenly sad. "Does Adam use it often?"

"Occasionally. When my mother's here, or sometimes cook watches with him, or I do when I have a chance. He doesn't like to be in there alone."

Gilly shifted in the seat until she faced Joe more fully. Her oval face was filled with concern. "Well, I can't blame him, Joe. Kids like to be around people, even if it's

51

strangers in a public theater. Do you think that's wise—isolating Adam like that?" Her arm curved over the back of the car seat as she tried to read the look on Joe's face. What she saw was unexpected; a tight, composed mask covering his handsome features. When he spoke, his words were so low she wouldn't have heard had she not been listening so intently.

"Adam will be fine. And safe."

"But you can't build a cage around him, Joe."

"Yes, I can, Gilly." The solemnity of his words was followed by an imposing silence. Gilly knew that there wasn't anything else to be said on the subject.

Surely he didn't mean that the way it sounded, Gilly thought, reluctantly focusing on the passing countryside. Joe Bennett was a kind, sensitive man, if a bit rigid at times. And he was obviously devoted to Adam. After all, no other father, divorced or not, had stepped forth to help with the boys! No, surely she'd misunderstood. . . .

Joe's thoughts had quickly passed beyond a subject that didn't lend itself to discussion and on to more pressing, close-at-hand matters, namely one Gilly Holmes.

Damn, it was nice having her there beside him! He stretched one hand over the back of the passenger's seat and wove his fingers through the thick waves of her ponytail.

"Well, Gilly, tell me, what's a nice girl like you doing in a job like this?" He looked at her out of the corner of his eye.

"Den mother?" Gilly laughed. "Goes with the territory, Joe."

"The territory being—"

"Timmy."

Joe noticed the soft smile that accompanied the name.

"Timmy wanted to be a scout, and there wasn't anyone else, so I ignored the fact that I didn't know beans about scouting and jumped in. And it's a lot of fun! I like being with the kids."

"Gilly, you're not afraid of much, are you?" The question had popped out of nowhere, a simple observation of this woman who faced life so squarely.

Gilly's throaty laugh circled the car. "Oh, my, Joe, you haven't been around me much. Sure I'm afraid of things. Who isn't?"

"You hide it well."

"I don't try to." Her blue eyes deepened to indigo as she searched his face and tried to find the reason for his question. "I don't think you're seeing courage or bravery, Joe. It's much less dramatic, I'm afraid. I've learned what I want out of life—and work at getting it. See?" She smiled and wrinkled her nose. "No Wonder Woman here at all."

Joe smiled and arched his brows. "Oh, I wasn't trying to make you Wonder Woman. I'm just not used to ladies who manage their own lives as well as you do."

Gilly shifted in the seat and looked intently out the window as the city sped by.

"Was that the wrong thing to say, Gilly?" Joe's fingers moved beneath her hair and gently massaged her neck.

Why is it so difficult to think with the feel of his hand on my neck? Her answer came slowly. "No, Joe. You're right. . . . Managing my own life is very important to me." Tiny prickles of pleasure traveled down Gilly's back. Dispelling it with a slight shrug of her shoulder she lifted her chin, lightened her voice, and changed the subject.

"Tell me about your mother, Joe. She's a terrific, made-to-order grandmother!"

"Yes, she's very good with Adam. He loves it when she visits."

"Which is often," Gilly remembered.

"Right!" Joe laughed. "Mother lives in a small town

53

outside Pittsburgh and I've often tried to get her to move here, since she seems to spend so much time going back and forth. There isn't any family left there now, but she's mighty hard to budge." He shook his head, the thick, dark hair lifting off his forehead. "She can't seem to leave the old frame house, or her quilting group or the church circle or the ninety-year-old lady down the street who depends on Mother to help with her canning. . . ."

Gilly's brows raised at the inner edges as she tried to imagine Joe coming from such a background. "Oh, I see. . . . So you weren't born with a silver spoon in your mouth?"

"No, Gilly, no silver spoon. A very tarnished garage-sale model would have been more apt. My parents didn't have a penny to play with. Dad worked his life away in the steel mill until it killed him."

There was a roughness to his voice that made Gilly wince. His hand slipped from her neck back to the wheel. "But your mother has certainly come through it all with a positive outlook, Joe. She doesn't look like a woman who led an unhappy life. Just the opposite, in fact."

"Yes, I suppose she did. But it could have been so much better. . . ." Joe's words faded off as he turned the corner of Gilly's street and concentrated on finding her house amid the row of look-alike frame bungalows. The quiet street was bathed in the darkening shadows of dusk as he pulled the car up to the curb in front of the house surrounded by bushy yellow marigold plants.

"Hmmm, looks like we're here." Joe said in surprise. "Didn't seem to take as long this time." He didn't want to leave. Not yet. Why hadn't he managed to get lost on the freeway?

"Yes." Gilly pushed a stray hair from her cheek with the back of her fingers. She looked at Joe and smiled. "Thank you." Then, feeling suddenly that there had to be more to say, she added quickly, "I promise you, Joe, that

54

not all our den meetings are as active as this one. . . ."
Gilly's sentence drooped in the middle.

Joe had turned the ignition off and the air inside the car was still. Suddenly there were no noisy cubs to distract them, no passing landscapes to comment on, no camping crises. Only each other, and the awareness of it made Gilly feel unexpectedly ill at ease.

"I . . . I guess I'd better be going in. I've got to finish those comps I was working on. And I'm sure you have things to do as well."

Joe shook his head. Suddenly he had nothing to do or think about—no million-dollar company to worry about, no responsibilities, no pressures—only Gilly Holmes in her powder-blue warm-up, surrounded by a deep, moonlit night. He reached out and ran his fingers across the back of her hand.

His touch rippled across her skin, and Gilly shivered.

"Are you cold?" he asked, his brows drawing together.

Gilly lifted her head and looked at him intently, her eyes matching the night. She raised one hand in the air, a small smile curling the edges of her lips. "I'm baffled, Joe —not cold. You're having a very unexpected effect on me, and I'm not quite sure what to do about it." Her eyelashes swept across her cheeks as she swallowed around the lump building in her throat.

"Funny you should mention that. I feel a bit strange myself." Joe felt the fleecy softness of her warm-up as he rubbed it gently between his fingers. "It feels kind of nice, Gilly. Been a long time since I've wanted to catch stars. . . ." His breath stroked her cheek.

Joe began gently to massage her neck and shoulders. His fingers worked in strong, methodical movements, back and forth, across her shoulder and around the back curve of her neck. She was lovely. Lovely and magical and capable of erasing his rational world in a breath.

"Joe, I—" Gilly raised her head, but the words were

lost as Joe's lips slowly and firmly covered her own. His kiss was gentle at first, soft as the filmy moonlight filtering through the open window. Gilly didn't move. Her lips were still, her hands folded like a schoolgirl's in her lap.

Joe wove his fingers gently into her hair, easing her head closer toward him. He felt more daring now, more convinced that kissing Gilly Holmes was not only a delicious thing to do, but somehow very right. His lips moved persuasively against hers until he felt the slight resistance she had offered begin to disappear.

"Feels good. . . ." Gilly murmured in the tiny space between them as she allowed herself a quick breath of air.

"And who are we to protest nature, right, Gilly?"

Joe's voice was husky as it feathered her cheek. Bowing his head slightly, he brushed her neck with a light kiss, then lifted up to taste her lips again.

Lightning streaks surged through Gilly's whole body as she kissed him back, tentatively at first, then with a passion born of his touch.

Her body shifted naturally in his embrace as his arm cradled her, one hand gently cupping her head. She felt fragile in his arms, vulnerable, and Joe smiled into her soft, hazy gaze.

Tiny streams of moonlight fell onto her hair, painting auburn highlights into the waves, and Joe's breath caught in his throat; something in Gilly Holmes was touching his heart. He could feel it as keenly as the silky coolness of her hair on his cheek. Fighting the urge to carry her inside, Joe kissed her again, then drew slightly apart.

"Gilly."

Gilly's hand lifted to his chest, then pushed slightly as she sought some space between them. "I know, Joe, you don't have to say anything. We let the moonlight get to us." She gulped in a deep breath of air and smiled into his dark eyes. "I should have stopped you, but you know"—

56

her eyes sparkled like a very young girl's—"it felt very nice. There was something in me that wanted you to kiss me very much. So don't be embarrassed or—"

"Embarrassed!" Joe exclaimed, twisting uncomfortably in the seat. "Gilly, that's one thing I sure as hell don't feel. I feel *other* things"—he looked at her out of the corners of his flashing black eyes—"but definitely not embarrassment."

Gilly took a deep breath, calming the butterflies swirling wildly inside her stomach. "I only meant you shouldn't feel . . ."

"Shouldn't feel what, Gilly?" He watched her intently. "I feel great! Matter of fact, *you* feel great." His hand slipped beneath the loose collar of her sweatshirt.

Gilly took a deep breath of chilled autumn air and scolded herself fiercely. *Come on, Gilly, since when have you had trouble handling men?* Her emotions fought back. *But I don't want to handle this man. I want the wonderful feel of his lips, the warmth he sends shooting through my body. I want to press close to him and feel his heartbeat beneath my hands. . . .*

Gilly! The bright smile that flashed across her face was as forced as it looked. "I really do have to go in now, Joe." Before she could change her mind, Gilly slipped over to the edge of the seat and quickly opened the car door. The cool breeze steadied her as she stood straight on the sidewalk. She paused for a moment and breathed deeply. There. Everything was fine again. Normal. She turned back toward the car and spoke brightly. "Good night, Joe."

"Gilly." Joe was out of the car and beside her in an instant. "About tomorrow—"

"Tomorrow?" Gilly shook her head. Maybe she wasn't as steady yet as she had thought. She smiled softly at Joe. "Tomorrow . . . is Saturday. . . ."

"Yes."

Gilly frowned in the chill autumn air and wondered when she'd be thinking clearly again. She smiled softly at Joe. "I don't understand."

"Tomorrow is a whole long day of lovely moments, which we shall fill together. I thought an early dinner and the new Neil Simon play . . ." He lifted the long, thick shimmer of hair from between her shoulders and cradled it possessively in the palm of his hand.

The fog lifted slowly and Gilly's brows drew together in a puzzling frown. *Her* tomorrow. Joe was filling her hours and minutes! "Oh, that tomorrow. I'm sorry, Joe, but Saturdays are very busy for me. I'm usually bushed at the end of the day." Caution, nurtured diligently over the years, made Gilly step back. "Perhaps another time."

"I know you're bushed. And that's why you need a night out, Gilly."

Joe's voice was very serious now, and Gilly tried to quiet the uneasy feeling that began to nibble away at the edge of her consciousness. The heat of his touch still filled her, sending crazy messages to her brain. Joe Bennett blurred her thinking processes. She forced another smile. "Thanks, Joe. But we—Timmy and I—usually just crash in front of the television on Saturday nights. Takeout Chinese food, a half-gallon of double fudge ice cream, and we're *very* relaxed." She laughed more sincerely now but stopped when Joe stepped closer and slowly traced his finger over her cheekbone.

"Chinese food—that's a terrific idea. Our club has a wonderful Chinese special. We'll take the boys. Is seven o'clock all right?"

Gilly looked up at the moon and tried to separate the feelings stirring inside her.

Joe's hand moved up beneath her hair, and the gentle pressure of his touch increased just enough to scatter the clear, logical workings of her mind. Her eyes moved to a bright, flickering star a billion miles away, closed for a brief moment, then settled back into Joe's waiting gaze.

He met her look with a grin and raised three fingers to his brow. "I'm safe, cub-scout honor."

Laughter bubbled up Gilly's throat and she brought a finger to his lips. "Shhh, before you blaspheme any further!" She took a step away. "We'll be ready at seven."

And she hurried up the walkway, hoping the crunch of crisp leaves beneath her feet blotted out the sound of her pounding heart.

CHAPTER FOUR

"Well, Gilly dear, tell me what you think. Yellow is definitely one of my colors, isn't it?" Mary Bennett smoothed the blue skirt and straightened the collar on her canary-yellow den-leader's blouse with one hand while she deftly maneuvered the wheel of Joe Bennett's shiny van with the other.

Gilly lifted her sunglasses off her nose and turned sideways on the seat to scrutinize Mary's appearance with feigned exactness. In just three short weeks she had become very fond of Mary Bennett, and when she had insisted on filling in for Joe as Gilly's assistant, Gilly had enthusiastically agreed. After staying up most of the night working on a layout, she was especially appreciative of her help today. She grinned in approval. "Mary, I think you look terrific. The ideal den mother!"

Mary laughed heartily. "At sixty-two years old? There's nothing ideal at this age, dear, thank you just the same. But no matter. I'm having the time of my life!"

"Mary, how much farther is it?" Her question was echoed by the rambunctious cub scouts in the back of the van.

"Oh, not far, Gilly. We'll be there in two shakes of a lamb's tail." Mary's eyes sparkled.

Gilly's enthusiasm was considerably more subdued. "And you're sure this is all right? I mean, you really want to do this?" *Gilly* wasn't sure about it at all. Shuttling the entire cub den into Joe's office for a field trip didn't exactly seem Joe Bennett's cup of tea. "I know how busy Joe is, and somehow this seems an imposition, something Joe—"

Mary's gray head was bobbing to the bumps in the road. "Now, you stop worrying! Of course I'm sure. This is a perfect place for the boys to earn their computer elective. Besides, it'll make Adam proud to show off Joe's shop. He needs that, you see. They *both* do. Joseph is a very loving father, Gilly, but sometimes he doesn't exactly know how to handle that love. . . ."

Her voice trailed off, and Gilly's thoughts immediately turned to Joe. They'd been doing that a lot lately—in the middle of working late on a layout, in the supermarket, while phoning the dentist, and at Timmy's soccer games. . . . The Chinese dinner had been a fun night for everyone, even when Timmy and Adam insisted on using chopsticks for everything including the won ton soup, and the laughing group was there to see the kitchen close four hours later. The next day he'd sent Timmy a wok with his own set of real chopsticks and a lovely fan for her. Gilly smiled at the memory.

And a few nights later Joe had shown up at her door with a huge bouquet of daisies and yellow roses—to match her floor, he'd said—and whisked her away to a wonderful little seafood restaurant where just the two of them had stuffed themselves with fresh clams and oysters as they watched the moon cast lovely shadows on the black, clear river beyond the windows. But it was the taste of his kiss that had lasted far longer than that of the succulent seafood. . . .

"Well, men, we're here!" Mary announced as she turned the van into a parking lot adjacent to the Bennett Building. With the sureness of a drill sergeant she had the cubs out of the van, their shirts tucked neatly into their pants, and was leading them into the spacious reception area of Joe's offices.

"Hello, Myra. Good afternoon, Gloria." Mary Bennett bustled around the lovely area, obviously a familiar and welcome visitor. Smiling sweetly, she smelled bouquets of fresh flowers with delighted relish, asked abut newborn children and spouses and vacation plans.

Gilly stood near the door watching Mary's wonderful sweep of the office. She was quite a lady, strong but with a lovely sparkle beneath her smile. Her son was like her in some ways, yet also very different. Watching her work with the cub scouts Gilly had been inspired more than once by her marvelous openness to life. She approached everything with an unbridled excitement that was refreshing and stimulating all at once.

Joe, on the other hand, seemed to meet life with such caution it was sometimes startling. Adam's life was carefully charted and monitored, his activities screened more carefully than the President's. Even Mary had seemed irritated by Joe's behavior at times and had given in only after a fierce argument a week earlier when Joe refused to allow Adam to accompany the scouts to a construction site.

"Of all the damnable ideas!" he'd growled to both Mary and Gilly, his black eyes flashing. "A kid could be killed in two seconds down there!"

"But they'll be wearing hard hats," Mary had protested, "and be under the close supervision of the foreman. And the work under way is actually quite tame,

Joseph. They're building a one-story school, for heaven's sake."

"Tame for hardened construction workers," he'd bellowed until the hair stood up on Gilly's arms, "but not for my only son!" And the subject had been dropped and never brought up again.

Gilly shook her head softly at the memory. Joe Bennett might take her breath away, but he was certainly puzzling at times.

Mary's chirping voice drifted over from the other side of the room. "Now, Sam, you must meet Joe's good friend, Gilly Holmes."

Joe's good friend . . . that *did* sound good. . . . Straightening up she buried her thoughts and walked over to shake hands with a tall, mustached man who returned her smile generously.

"Hi, Gilly. I'm Joe's VP—Sam Harris. We're delighted to have you and . . . ah . . . the scouts here. Such a nice surprise!"

Gilly shot a look over at Mary, who was innocently rearranging a vase of marigolds. She looked back up at Sam. "Surprise? You didn't know we were coming?"

Sam laughed. "Well, *I* didn't, but that doesn't matter. Mary knows she's always welcome. Well, nice meeting you. Hope the kids enjoy the shop. Sorry I have to rush off, but our meeting's about to begin."

"Mary"—Gilly flew to Mary's side—"I don't think this is—"

"No, it's not." Mary beamed agreeably. "You're absolutely right! Lounging in the lobby is not the place for these young 'uns. They want to see the *real* stuff. Come along, Gilly!" With a decisive wave of her hand Mary bustled on ahead, collecting the boys in a raggedy line and ushering them firmly down the hall.

Gilly had no recourse but to follow, but she knew as soon as she spotted the whirring, clicking computer room that it had been a bad idea to come, computer elective or not!

Like bees to honey the boys traveled through the door and over to the blinking screens, playground-stained fingers itching for a feel of the keys.

"Hey, this is terrific!" Tim screeched, his eyes round as saucers as he sought out Adam. "Boy, are you lucky to have a dad with all this!"

Adam grinned lopsidedly. "Yeah, it's cool, I guess. My dad lets me work the computers sometimes if I'm careful. But it sure is more fun having you guys with me!"

"Hey, where is your dad, anyway?"

Gilly listened to the exchange and realized she was wondering the same thing. Where *was* Joe? Suddenly she shivered. The answer was as clear as the goose bumps on her arm. He didn't know they were coming! She quickly looked around. The boys were standing beside a computer, watching a good-natured young man punch in numbers. Joe was nowhere to be seen.

Well, at least things are going smoothly. She let her breath out slowly, tentatively, as if every breath might be her last. *The boys are doing okay. Perhaps we can get out without a mishap, and Joe will never even know his quiet operation was invaded by nine little Indians!*

As the demonstration neared its end, Gilly glanced over at Adam's face and was further convinced that the trip might have some merits to it. The small boy was grinning from ear to ear as he slid onto a chair and showed his friends how to program their names. Gilly smiled. She'd like to see his face light up like that more often. The shuffling of tennis shoes indicated the demonstration had about run its course, and Gilly stepped up before the group.

"Okay, fellas, that's it. Now let's thank the gentleman —*and* Adam—for letting us come—and head to the Ice Cream Shoppe for those sundaes Mary promised you!"

"Just one more stop, Gilly dear," Mary piped up from the corner. "Sam Harris says there's a planning meeting going on that would be *wonderful* for the youngsters to see. It will just take a minute." And she quickly paraded the boys out the door, down a wide hallway, and around the corner.

Gilly's breath caught in her throat. Joe! He'd certainly be at the planning meeting. *Joe, the corporate president.* Her eyes brightened, intrigued by the thought, then just as quickly flashed in dismay. *Joe the corporate president, being unexpectedly visited by a cub-scout troop!*

"Wait!" Gilly gasped aloud as she spun on her heels and raced after the crooked line of bodies. "No, don't go in there!"

The scouts stopped just as they reached the open door, their eyes darting between Mary and Gilly.

"Mary, I really don't think it's a good idea," she said in hushed tones, her words traveling up to the smiling woman at the front of the line.

Mary paused for just a moment, then winked at Gilly over the scouts. "It's all right, Gilly dear. Trust me." And she proceeded to tap each boy gently on the shoulder, ushering him into the room.

Gilly slowly shook her head. Mary Bennett was as difficult to budge as her son! She caught her breath, forced a smile neatly in place on her flushed face, and slipped silently through the doorway.

Mary had taken center stage.

"Hello, Joseph. Please excuse our little interruption, but we'll be quiet as church mice! Don't you pay any attention to us." Her voice rang out loud and clear as she turned to usher the rest of the boys into place, explaining the meeting to them softly.

"Now, boys, you'll see how a planning meeting is run. And this will count for a career elective."

Joe Bennett sat at the head of the long, polished oval

table, his hands resting on a black leather notebook. Three people sat on each side of the table, disbelief written on their faces.

Gilly gulped, Mary smiled brightly, and Tim shouted, "Hi, Mr. Bennett. Sure is a terrific place you got here!"

Adam smiled happily into his father's black eyes, his hands shoved into his blue-jeans pockets. "Hi, Dad."

Joe rose slowly, his face unreadable. "Well, this is a . . . surprise." He looked slowly around the room, his lips a fine, controlled line.

Gilly's gaze fell to the floor. He had a right to be angry! He was running a business, after all, and had had no idea they were coming. She looked up and saw his eyes narrowing, focusing intently on her face. Gilly wanted to run, to turn into a speck of dust and disappear from the face of the earth, or at least the Bennett Computer Company! Instead she looked straight ahead, concentrating on a tiny spot above Joe's head. Finally his gaze shifted from her face and she relaxed enough to follow his eyes.

They fastened firmly on Mary Bennett, and held there as he spoke. "You all know Adam and my mother . . . and now, it seems, you're about to meet Adam's cub-scout den—as well as his lovely leader."

Everyone nodded agreeably at the small boy and the vivacious gray-haired lady, and then they all stared at Gilly Holmes, who was trying to reduce her height considerably as she shifted her weight behind the tallest boy in the den. Her face burned as she felt the pull of Joe's stare that brought her eyes reluctantly up to his.

"Hello." She smiled weakly, her heart pounding wildly in her chest. She shifted her eyes to Mary. "Don't you think we ought to leave, Mary? I think Joe . . . Mr. Bennett is busy and—"

"Gracious, I am so sorry, Joseph! We only wanted the boys to see how computer programs were born." Mary's hands shot to her cheeks, the sparkle in her eyes as bright as ever.

Joe shook his head, a smile beginning in his eyes, then drawing up the edges of his mouth. He should have known. Mary Bennett would invade a summit meeting if it might interest her only grandson! "It's okay, Mother. We'll finish up in short order and I'll be right with you."

Mary nodded happily as the boys settled in, leaning against the walls and windowsills.

Gilly looked around to see if anyone had heard the relieved sigh that escaped her lips. Well, cub-scout meetings were more event-filled now that the Bennetts had fallen into her life! She settled back against the cool, paneled wall and took a slow breath. *Go with it, Gilly—relax and enjoy.*

And that meant freely watching Joe Bennett, quietly, unnoticed, across the crowded room. Her lips curved in a pleased smile as the old show tune hummed in her head and drew her eyes to Joe—and kept them there.

He sat comfortably in the leather chair, his broad shoulders relaxed, and he resumed his meeting, speaking to the group in cool, even tones.

Gilly found the room falling away, leaving only Joe framed there before her, his dark hair highlighted in blue-black streaks by the late-afternoon sunlight. His voice was all business, but his eyes held a shimmering light that seemed directed straight at Gilly.

The quick opening of a door and shuffling of footsteps scattered her portrait, and Gilly looked toward the noise, a wave of disappointment settling in as the images faded.

Gloria, the secretary Gilly had seen earlier, hurried over to Joe's side, and she listened with half an ear as snatches of IBM, programs, and sales figures larger than her life filtered through the air. Joe spoke with firm command, answering the woman's questions and circling items on the sheets of paper in front of him. When Gloria walked out, it was obvious to everyone in the room that the Bennett Company had made another sale, a huge one to a computer giant, that left the small, privately owned company standing tall in the world of silicon chips and complicated hardware.

The announcement was made, applauded, and the meeting resumed. Joe was in complete control. Joe Bennett the professional, Joe Bennett the executive. Gilly marveled at the ease with which he slipped into this role, as if born to it. He was so powerful, Gilly thought. A powerful, handsome enigma . . . and with enough sensuality to light up more than computers! Gilly shook her head to scatter her thoughts. *Cub scouts! Pay attention to your cub scouts!*

From his vantage point at the head of the table, Joe watched the sunlight bounce off Gilly's hair as her head moved slowly back and forth. He hadn't the faintest idea why she was shaking her head no to Sam Harris's suggestion that they speed up production of the new program, but it didn't really matter. All that mattered just then was her presence in his boardroom.

The talk around him blurred into a hum as he watched her standing there, a strange wave of excitement easing itself into his bones. An unfamiliar feeling, to be sure. Joe Bennett's life was orderly, protected, filled with the dealings of big business that kept Bennett Company growing —and other parts of the world safely at bay—but the excitement Gilly stirred in him was new. New, and as welcome as sunlight in the dead of winter. He shifted in the chair, feeling an uncomfortable, heated stirring deep inside himself.

At that moment the subdued business air was broken by one of the scout's sudden onslaught of hiccups. The feeling inside Joe began to subside. *Just in time too!* he thought.

Grinning kindly at the embarrassed cub scout, now

beet red with two hands clasped firmly over his mouth, Joe stood.

"Well, it looks like we've covered about everything, ladies and gentlemen. We've sure enjoyed having you men"—he nodded at the suddenly quiet scouts—"and as for the rest of us, I think we'll call it quits for today. I'll see you all here again on Monday. Same time."

The planning committee filed out to the tune of the boys' outpouring of pent-up giggles over Jerry O'Hara's hiccups.

"Gosh, Adam"—Tim Holmes pulled his friend to the side as the others left the room. He spoke in a library whisper, his hand tight on Adam's arm—"you're just about the luckiest kid I know! And your dad too. My mom has to work on the dining-room table!" His blue eyes flashed with unabashed envy.

"Lucky? Yeah . . . I guess." Adam scratched his head.

Timmy's voice grew with his enthusiasm. "And I bet your dad lets you come down here and play anytime you want! Well, sometimes I get to use my mom's pens and stuff, but that's kinda boring."

"Yeah," Adam looked around the room as if seeing it for the first time. "I guess it's great. Yeah, we come down here together on Saturdays and I get to do stuff on the computers and"—his voice began to pick up—"yeah, Tim. Hey, what did your dad do?"

Tim twisted his yellow neckerchief between his fingers as Gilly walked up behind him. "Oh, he did stuff. I dunno. He took me to carnivals, I remember, and on picnics and to the zoo 'cause he didn't have to go to an office much. And once he got me a pony for my birthday."

Gilly cringed from her silent post behind the boys. This was what she had worked so hard to foster—*good* memories that would fill Timmy's mind with lovely thoughts of his father. And they were all true, all accurate, but told so little of the whole story, of the things Craig Holmes *didn't* give his tiny son, such as security and dependability. Why, Craig had been little more than an overgrown boy himself, Timmy's beloved friend, a sweet tempered but undependable pal.

"Wow!" Adam's face lit up the nearly empty room with envy. "I sure wish my dad had *that* kind a job! He doesn't have time for that sorta stuff. He only cares—"

Gilly had tried to be invisible, but her efforts suddenly flew out the window. She placed a hand gently on Adam's shoulder. "Adam, your father is a wonderful man— and I know you're very proud of him. Why"—Gilly laughed lightly—"how many other fathers let the whole scout den visit their office? Or go on very rainy camp-outs?"

"Yeah." Adam's head bobbed slowly in polite agreement. "Sure . . ." He glanced quickly over at Tim, the envious excitement creeping back into his voice. "But it sure would be great to have a pony. I never even had a dog!"

"Well, perhaps someday we can go riding out at Kahn's Stables and you can get the feel of a horse beneath you." Gilly ruffled the youngster's hair as she spoke.

"I don't think so." Joe Bennett's low, controlled voice preceded him back into the boardroom. "But we can talk about that at home." The statement was directed toward Adam, and the subject closed in a fraction of a second.

When he looked over at Gilly, the serious edge was gone from his voice, his mouth curved in a smile. "Well, Gilly, how did you like the shop?"

Thoughts of Adam and ponies and hiccups all fused together, then disappeared beneath his disarming look.

"I liked it, Joe. Thanks for being so gracious. I have a feeling we were a bit of a surprise." He slipped an arm over her shoulder and guided her across the room, a polite, friendly gesture that caused her heart to jump.

Joe laughed. "Perhaps. But it was a nice surprise. And you know, I never noticed before seeing you in the boardroom, that you had freckles. Just a few. Right here—" He turned and traced across her cheekbones and over her nose. "They're charming."

As her blush deepened, Gilly's eyes darted toward the door. The boys had disappeared. Thank heavens for that! What was getting into Joe?

"Well, yes," she said quickly. "There are a few there and other—" She stopped quickly.

"Go on, Gilly. There are a few there . . . and other places?" Joe's eyes sparkled with interest.

Gilly tossed her head, wondering how *anyone* could possibly find herself in a lavish, dignified corporate office, discussing freckles!

"Nothing more to be said about my freckles, Joe. But this really is a fascinating place." There, she'd gotten out of that without much damage. Smiling brightly, she went on. "Now, where do you suppose the group is? Mary and I are headed for the Ice Cream Shoppe."

"Don't worry about a thing." Joe followed her through the doorway. "My mother will take care of the kids. I'll drive you home."

Gilly glanced at her watch. "Oh, no, Joe. Mary and I are—"

"Mother said she can handle them alone. I told her I'd drive you home. The workday's almost over anyway. And I need some fresh air."

Not nearly as much as I do! Gilly shook her head slowly, hoping the fog would lift. His hand was on her arm and the warmth it sent curling through her body was quite overwhelming.

"Joe, listen, maybe another time—"

But he was already guiding her down the long hallway,

then out into the spacious lobby. Joe looked around the room. "Looks like they've left. Listen, Gilly, my mother instigated this trip, and she can handle those boys just fine. As you've seen, she can handle just about anything."

"And it looks like you've inherited that trait. . . ." Gilly felt utterly confused. "You know, Joe, I don't like things being arranged for me. I wish you hadn't sent her off like that."

"Sent her off?" Joe's laugh was low and rich. "Gilly, no one sends Mary Bennett anywhere! Don't let her fool you. It just so happens that *this* time I agreed with her. Now, what'll it be, a ride with me or a long walk home?"

CHAPTER FIVE

Gilly Holmes was far too tired to walk.

"I have an overwhelming feeling of déjà vu," she murmured, stepping into Joe's car.

"Oh?" Joe slipped out of his suit jacket and set it in the back of the car, then started the engine.

"Yes—getting into this car, having you drive me home, leaving your mother to look after my responsibilities."

"She loves it! Besides, she agrees with me that you work too hard. You shouldn't be trying to run your business all alone."

"I'm not all alone. I have Tugg."

"Yes, Tugg." Joe liked Tugg, but it was damn irritating that Tugg was able to spend more time with Gilly than he could! "Maybe you need to hire more people. You're a mother, too, Gilly. That in itself is—"

"And you're a father, Joe. That doesn't keep you away from the office now, does it? And how can I possibly hire more people when Tugg and I are just barely making ends meet?" The tiredness she'd been fighting off after her late night was now returning full force. And the day was far from over. She still had the late shift at the restaurant where she hostessed on occasion. At least Tugg would be at home to baby-sit for Tim.

Joe threw her a quick glance. "Sure, I'm a father, Gilly. But I have others to help me. You do everything yourself."

"Well, that's the way it has to be."

"No, it isn't. I could help, Gilly. Take my cook—mother won't let her near the kitchen while she's here. Why don't you use her, and—"

Gilly's tiredness was eased by the slow laughter that began in her center and spread outward. "Oh, Joe, you are, as your mother would say, a 'caution.'"

The serious expression on his face never wavered. "No, listen! It makes perfect sense. I'm paying her to do nothing, and she hates it. She's so anxious to get back to the helm again, she's starting to overfeed the birds!"

"Joe, just where would I fit a cook in my tiny kitchen?" She lifted one brow into her bangs, her lips quirking into a smile. "And how, pray tell, would she adjust to a stove with only one working burner, and a child whose favorite dinner is macaroni and cheese, and *only* the kind that comes out of a box!" Her laughter rippled on the breeze. She tilted her head to one side and looked at him, her blue eyes sparkling. "Thanks, Joe, but I think your cook would be very unhappy at the Holmes home. But I do appreciate the gesture. Men have given me flowers and candy before, but no one has *ever* offered me a cook!"

Joe grinned. "Okay, okay. You won that round. The cook might not work. Besides, she has a phobia about dogs. Henry would cause immediate hives. But there must be something I can do so you'll have more time for

74

yourself." *And for me, Gilly,* he added with silent resolve. *You need a lot more time for me. . . .*

"Joe"—Gilly's tone grew serious—"I appreciate your concern, but Tim and I get along fine. As a matter of fact, I'm proud of the fact that we manage as well as we do. It's taken me a while to get to this point, but I like managing my life, and I think I do a pretty good job!"

"I'm sure you do, Gilly." Joe looked over at her for a moment, then laughed. "Okay, I'll back off. But only on one condition. I happen to have it on good authority that your cupboard would shame Mother Hubbard. How about an early dinner?"

Gilly looked over at him, her heart swelling. He was awfully hard to resist. Besides, she was starving, and Joe was right on target—one can of tuna and assorted stale crackers weren't much to get excited about. *Tomorrow* she'd have time to market. . . . "Well, it's tempting, but Timmy is still with your mother and—"

"No problem. I'll call home. He can eat with Mom and Adam." Joe pointed to the dashboard and picked up the receiver of a portable phone.

Gilly grinned and shook her head. Things were so easy in Joe's world. "Okay, Joe. But just a hamburger, someplace very casual where a haggard-looking den mother won't scare off the other customers. And I have to be home in an hour or two."

Joe completed his phone call, then drew his attention back to Gilly. "A hamburger?" He groaned. "How about Angelo's? They have fantastic pastas—"

"Joe! The waiters wear tuxedoes at Angelo's. That's not casual!"

"Okay, Gillian, calm down. I've got another idea. Sure —it's perfect! Hang on." He turned the wheel and expertly guided the car into the right lane, then off the highway. One hand fell to her knee in a brief squeeze, then lingered there.

Gilly didn't move, just left it there, enjoying the warm connection. With a contented sigh, a soft smile curving her lips, she leaned her head back against the cool, soft leather.

Joe stole a glance at her and felt the familiar rush of pleasure pass through him. Even tired she was beautiful. Glancing beyond her through the window he spotted a neon sign and quickly pulled the car off the street and into the crowded parking lot.

Before Gilly quite comprehended where they were, Joe was out of the car and had disappeared inside the cinder-block building. HARRY'S FINE DRIVE-IN, the sign above it read. She peered through the glass and could see him moving into a line, his large, firm body moving surely and confidently. In minutes he returned, his arms wrapped around two huge sackfuls of food, and then they drove off. "Mission accomplished. Step one, anyway."

There was an uncharacteristic boyishness to his mood that made Gilly smile. "And step two?"

"Coming up, my dear."

In minutes Joe had joined the early-evening traffic headed for Fairmount Park.

"Joe, you surprise me." Gilly laughed. "If I were doing a profile on you, I don't think I would have included picnics at dusk in the park."

Joe smiled slowly. "One hundred percent accurate, Gilly. I've never done this before."

Gilly's head jerked up. "Never been on a picnic?" She thought of little Adam. "Really?"

"Not for a long time, anyway. Not since I was a kid."

"I see." Gilly was thoughtful. "And Harry's Fine Drive-in, then—it's not a regular spot?"

"I never saw it before. It simply appeared on the horizon just as your stomach began making those awful noises." His smile widened. "I think it's an omen."

"I hope it's digestible." Gilly laughed as the car came

to a stop in an isolated parking spot above the narrow Schuylkill River.

It was a part of the large city park Gilly hadn't been to before. She got out of the car and walked over to the beginning of a gentle slope that fell slowly down to the edge of the river. "This is lovely, Joe. Come look."

Propping the food bags up against a giant oak tree, Joe strode over to her. The slope led down to the water, where a grassy bank offered first-row seats for watching scullers slicing through the waters as they raced down the river. The land across the river was level, and from where they stood, Joe and Gilly could see the tops of the maples just beginning to turn a russet hue.

"It is nice. Strange that a place I pass nearly every day could be such a surprise."

"Surprises are nice." She slipped down onto the grass and pulled her knees up beneath her chin, her eyes inviting him to join her. Joe slid down, his long legs stretching out in front of him and his back resting on the smooth bark of a tree.

"They sure are. Especially those that come with eyes bluer than the sky and hair that's the color of autumn." Joe wrapped a silken strand around his finger and studied her, his black eyes smiling.

Gilly breathed deeply, then tilted her head toward Joe, her eyes locking into his. She'd like to stay there forever, with the soft grass tickling her legs and Joe beside her, warming her with his eyes. "I'm glad we came, Joe. I can almost feel all my weariness leaving me."

Joe smiled in response, then leaned forward and curled his fingers around the narrow bones of her shoulder. Gently and firmly he began to massage the tired muscles in her neck and shoulders.

"Hmmm—Joe, that's wonderful!" She closed her eyes and let the delicious sensations seep in deeply. "Where did you learn such an art?"

"I was a masseur in a great lady's home in a former life." His husky voice tickled her ear.

"I see," Gilly murmured. "Lucky lady. Should you ever go into the business again . . ." Her head fell to one side as Joe lifted her hair and kneaded the stiff muscles of her neck.

"Oh, I intend to."

His long fingers caressed each tender spot across her shoulders, and Gilly decided hazily that heaven must be a little bit like this. Perfect, delicious contentment.

Joe stopped massaging just as Gilly was about to fall asleep. "I suppose it's time we put Harry to the test and tried these burgers."

"I guess you're right." Reluctantly she reached over and grabbed the bag. "Do masseurs eat?"

"Constantly," Joe growled. "How do you suppose these fingers got so strong?" Joe wiggled them beneath her nose, then grabbed a hamburger and took a large bite. "Hey, they're not bad!"

Gilly swallowed a bite. "Mine's great. But then I've rarely met a hamburger I didn't like." She giggled softly. "And that's fortunate, because next to tuna and macaroni, hamburgers keep Tim and me fat and happy."

Her comment drew his eyes immediately to her body and Gilly squirmed beneath his slow, devouring look. She should never have worn a skirt on the field trip! Trying to sit comfortably on the grass without having it rise nearly to her hips was becoming a problem, and Joe's look didn't help. "I didn't mean it literally, Joe, so you can quit the analysis! She slapped him playfully on the knee and set a sack of fries in his lap. They ate in silence for a moment, then Gilly shifted and looked directly into Joe's face. "Joe, may I ask you something personal?"

Joe smiled. "Like vital statistics?"

"No. Like who is Adam's mother and what is she like?"

78

Joe shifted beneath her gaze, but his answer came readily, almost as if he'd been waiting for the question. "Patricia. Her maiden name was Lathrup." He watched Gilly for a reaction. There was none, and he continued. "Stanley Lathrup was one of the wealthiest investors in Philadelphia, until his company suddenly filed bankruptcy."

"Oh." Gilly bent her head and took another bite of her sandwich. *I don't care about her father, Joe. I want to know how she could ever leave that beautiful little boy. . . . I want to know if you loved this woman, Joe.*

Joe leaned his head back. "But you don't really give a damn about Stanley's ill-fated financial wizardry, do you, Gilly?" He reached over and wound a strand of her hair around his finger. "Except it *does* help explain Patricia. We met when I was doing some consulting for her father. She had him invite me home for dinner one night." He laughed lightly. "Just like in the movies. I was a kind of novelty to Patricia, a young, cocky kid from a working-class family who wasn't afraid of much, including her father."

Gilly watched carefully for signs of hurt. Joe had suffered badly somewhere along the line. Was it Patricia? His calm eyes gave no clue.

"Anyway, to make a long story short, she thought she loved me, although"—he grinned at Gilly—"I suppose it was just my body. When we returned from our honeymoon, Stanley had filed for bankruptcy. The endless allowances were gone, so were the fancy trips. I had started my business then, but it was just a basement operation and money was scarce." He picked up a cup and rolled it gently between his hands. "She was used to silver platters and I gave her paper plates." He looked over at Gilly. "It didn't work out, so we divorced."

"But *Adam*, Joe," Gilly blurted out. "What about Adam?"

79

Joe looked startled for a moment, his face clouding over briefly. "Adam? Adam's everything to me. Patricia went along with me, and had a baby." His voice dropped. "But it didn't solve any problems. She left. She's not a bad person, Gilly. And I suppose she has some sort of feeling for him, although I don't like it when she suddenly decides to come into his life for brief moments. Those are few and far between, though. She found a rich man to marry who likes to travel. So she's happy. . . ."

But she doesn't want that beautiful, loving child? Gilly thought sadly.

"Some people don't want children, you know. It really doesn't make Patricia bad. She tried, but didn't have a lot to build on. Her parents gave her the world on a platter. It was hard to get used to anything different, like being a mother. I think at times she wished it were different. But then, I wasn't too open back then, couldn't deal with much myself. It was a tremendous relief when she walked out of our lives."

His voice broke off and Gilly could sense the agony within him. She knew Joe had gone as far as he could for now. Pulling another hamburger out of the bag she thrust it into his hands and smiled. "Well, no matter who got you started in your company, you've done a wonderful job with it, Joe." She watched the evening shadows slant across the rugged planes of his face. "You must be very proud."

Joe took a long swig of Coke from a foam cup. He looked surprised. "Proud? I don't think much about that. I'm satisfied. I wanted to build a company that would be very successful. This one is. I've gotten from it what I wanted to get."

"But you proved yourself, and your ability. You must be proud of that!"

"I never cared about proving myself. I *knew* what ability I had." He half smiled. "Remember, I was a cocky kid

80

who thought the world was there for me. After . . . after Patricia left, all I wanted was a company that made a lot of money. And I got it. So I'm content, not proud really."

Gilly's brows lifted. "That sounds so . . . so . . ."

"Crass? Materialistic? It is." Joe was flippant. "And it's also very boring." He stretched his arms above his head and shook his head back and forth as if banishing the past. When he looked at Gilly again, his eyes were focused only on her. "Gillian Holmes is much more interesting. So tell me, *who* is Gilly Holmes?"

Gilly laughed. "And what is she doing eating *three* hamburgers!" She stared in sudden amazement at the pile of wrappers strewn about her legs.

"Freudian. Oral gratification."

Gilly laughed, and Joe grew serious again. "Gilly, when did your husband die?"

The abruptness of the question startled Gilly. She answered quickly. "Almost four years ago."

"That's not a very long time."

"It was a lifetime ago, Joe."

She didn't sound sad or self-pitying, merely matter of fact, and the emotionless tone of her voice surprised Joe. "I suppose it seems that way to you and Timmy."

"It doesn't just seem that way, it *is* that way. My life with Craig Holmes is so far removed from the present that I look upon it as another life, almost like a former incarnation. You know"—she forced a lightness into her voice—"like when you were busy rubbing that voluptuous lady's back."

"I can't quite tell whether you think that is good or bad."

"I think it's great! Especially since you preserved the talent—"

Joe brushed aside her diversion. "*Craig*, Gilly. Is it good it was a lifetime ago?"

Gilly smiled softly. "I don't want to pass judgment, Joe. But I'm doing quite nicely in this life, thank you."

"Were you and Craig happy?"

That question should have sent Gilly running for her life. Weaving her fingers through her thick hair she looked out over the rippling river and wondered briefly why she wasn't. The answer was obvious—set as clearly as day in the deep, caring tone that carried his question. She kept her eyes focused on a distant boat. "Yes, Joe. Craig and I *were* happy. We were the ideal couple: young, idealistic, a beautiful baby boy to share our life with." She smiled absently, remembering. They had been happy. For a while.

"I was a dutiful housewife, staying home, planting the garden, taking Timmy for wonderful walks in the park. And more often than not Craig joined me on our outings. He always seemed to have time for us." Gilly paused.

"Whenever I questioned how he could be away from the office so often, he'd hush me. I wasn't to bother my pretty little head about such things, he'd say with a grin. And then he'd come home the next day with a pony for Tim, or tickets for a trip, just to prove that he really *could* take care of everything."

Joe watched her carefully as she talked. Her eyes were as blue as the deepening sky, but filled with a distant sadness. "Gilly, it's okay. Perhaps I had no right to ask."

She turned and smiled. "Perhaps you didn't, but it's okay, Joe. It has worked out all right for Timmy and me. When Craig had his heart attack, I was devastated. I was just a child, in a way; he'd always taken care of everything. I'd never even paid a bill! And then I found out that he hadn't paid too many either. Craig had built a fairyland for us—a wonderful world that had about as much connection with reality as Timmy's toy trains! He died with debts that seemed they'd never end, with business obligations he'd never even attempted to meet." Her voice had softened, but she continued talking, her eyes moving from the river to Joe's, then back again. "So Timmy and I started to rebuild. I worked, paid off debts, and went to school. When I graduated in graphic design, Tugg and I set up shop. End of story." She looked over at Joe and smiled, dusky shadows of the setting sun playing across her face.

Gilly was quietly aware that Joe had moved closer again, and his arm now gently cradled her back.

But she couldn't see his dark eyes flashing with emotion. When he finally spoke, his voice was strained. "He left you with all that."

Gilly laughed softly. "All that, or nothing, depending on how you look at it. But he did love us, Joe."

"Then how could he have done such a damn foolish thing? The man was an idiot!" Joe's voice erupted with anger.

Gilly turned and put a hand on his knee. "No, Joe. He wasn't an idiot. The man was a boy. He never grew up, and his wife was a child who didn't know the difference."

The welcome movement of Joe's arm around her, pulling her back until she rested against the hard wall of his chest, was as natural as breathing. She rested her head on his shoulder. "But that child finally grew up, Joe." She tilted her head back to look into his eyes. "She's a woman now who can run her own life very nicely. I'm very proud of that, Joe, and I'll never, ever, let anyone put me in that vulnerable, painful position again."

Her last words were nearly hushed by the closeness of their lips, but the message echoed in Joe's head. It didn't make sense. None at all. Gilly Holmes needed someone, someone who would make absolute sure that she was never hurt again. She needed *him*.

Cupping her chin in the palm of one hand, he brought his lips down on hers, firmly and carefully sealing his resolve. Gilly's lips pressed back with gentle passion, one hand flat against the heat of his chest.

"Oh, Gilly," he whispered, "you are . . . very lovely to kiss." He ran a finger over the heated skin of her face, then dipped to claim her lips again. His tongue flicked teasingly over her bottom lip, then traced over the full curve of it before coaxing her lips apart.

Gilly fell back, her mind a blur. Her hand slid over his smooth chest as she kissed him again.

Then, with great effort, she pulled herself upright.

"Are you leaving?" Joe's eyes were hooded, his voice husky with desire.

Gilly ran a hand through her hair and felt her mind clear, then reluctantly glanced down at her wristwatch. "Yes, Joe. I have to get back. I have to work—"

Joe's finger traced over the gentle curve of her shoulder bones, then down over one breast.

Gilly shivered. "Stop it, Joe, or I'll never get home."

"Would you mind?" His finger moved slowly beneath the scooped collar of her blouse, pulling it carefully away from her skin.

Gilly backed away until his finger slipped out, then pulled herself up from the ground. Looking down at him she smiled warmly into his dark eyes. "I plead the fifth here, sir. Besides, what's important is that my bank balance would definitely mind. I need to work—"

"Day and night?" Joe's thick brows pulled together in a frown.

"Yes, tonight anyway." She picked up the bag and began cleaning up the remnants of their dinner.

Joe watched her for a moment, his hands folded behind his head as he leaned against the tree. Her hair fell over one shoulder as she bent to pick up scattered wrappings, and the way her breasts pushed against the soft fabric of her blouse delighted him. He wanted to pull her down on top of him, press her breasts against his chest, cradle her thighs between the palms of his hands. He yearned to feel the wonderful silkiness of her body, and he wondered about the fires Gilly Holmes had lit within him.

Shaking off the stirrings of arousal, he pulled himself off the ground until he towered over her.

Gilly looked up and their eyes locked together, then held there briefly as they each retreated into silence, toying with the thick emotions that held them there.

Finally Gilly pulled her eyes away. "It's dusk."

Joe looked out over the river. "Funny . . . it feels more like dawn." He looked down at Gilly and smiled, then wound his fingers through hers and together they walked back to the car.

CHAPTER SIX

Dear Friends,
Please come and help me celebrate my thirtieth (!) birthday.

I'd like all of you to join me in welcoming in another hope-filled year, and to thank each of you for your friendship, your laughter, your shoulders-to-cry-on these past few years, because it's all of you who have helped bring me to this day feeling so good about today, so hopeful about tomorrow.
See you Friday at eight!

Love,
Gilly

Gilly set the bright, cheerful card down on her dresser top and smiled. All printed—down to the stylized balloons that shadowed small, graceful brushes and easels and drawing boards. At the bottom was a sketch of a small boy hugging his soccer ball. It was all there: her son, her work. Her life.

She'd had such fun designing the cards and planning her own birthday thank-you bash. Even Timmy's playful teasing that kids over twelve don't have parties anymore couldn't dampen her enthusiasm.

This was special, this thirtieth birthday. Life was special once again.

Now all she needed to do was mail the cards and let Tugg know how many pizzas to bake, and she'd be all set.

As Gilly leafed absently through the stamped envelopes, her mind wandered from the party preparations, to the guest list, then landed with a heart-stopping lurch where they'd been all night: with Joe Bennett. Work had swept her up like a tornado this week, and she hadn't seen Joe since the day they'd been to Fairmount Park, even though he'd called each day and never strayed far from her thoughts.

The set to his chin, the crease in his cheek when he stopped her heartbeat with a smile, the proud line to his nose and the flashing blackness of his eyes—they were all there, all etched into her mind as clearly as a beloved painting. But Joe Bennett *wasn't* a painting. He breathed and walked, and touched her with a fiery caress that sent her emotions spinning off wildly on their own course. She seemed to have no control over the sensation. It rushed through her when she was showering, or fixing Timmy dinner, or when she sat quietly for a moment all by herself and tried to make sense out of it all.

She pulled his invitation from the pile and stared at his name and address. Threading through a bundle of anxious feelings was that unnerving warmth that spread and tangled through her like a vine.

How would Joe react to the invitation? All the others were old friends, and he hadn't met any of them except for Tugg. Maybe he wouldn't want to come, wouldn't feel comfortable with the others. The thought swept through her with a chill, then disappeared just as quickly. No. Somehow, at some moment she couldn't quite put her finger on, Joe Bennett had slipped firmly into her life. He would come. Because without him, how could she celebrate the present?

Dear, wonderful Joe, who swept her off her feet with a glance and held her there, suspended. Her brows lifted as she thought of him. *You do sweep me off my feet, Joe. And it feels so good for the moment, but I don't belong swirling through thin air, Joe. I'm no longer comfortable there, held up by another's arms. . . .*

She leaned her elbows on the smooth surface of the table, her eyes shifting from the card, to the mirror, then lingering on a small photo tucked into the frame. The corners had curled but the smiles were still intact: Timmy, Gilly, and Craig leaning over the edge of the Staten Island Ferry one summer vacation. The wind had whipped their hair into their laughing faces, and as she looked closer she could see that Timmy had lost his first tooth. Craig's grin matched Timmy's—carefree and innocent. But it was on her own face that her eyes lingered.

She stared hard at the image, her brows drawing together.

The young woman in the picture was smiling happily, her face held back to catch the breeze. Her brow was smooth as glass, her large eyes shining and clear and innocent. She was a storybook mother, young and lovely, a tiny, bright-eyed boy beside her, her husband's arm lingering on her shoulder in a protective gesture.

Gilly's eyes moved to the mirror. The woman who looked back resembled the photo image only superficially —same nose, same eyes. But the resemblance stopped there. Gilly laughed in surprise. "You've come a long way, baby."

It was as if two different artists had painted the pictures. The one in the mirror had features ripened by life: a sparkle in her eyes that spoke of determination and independence, and several soft, tiny lines that fanned out at each corner in laughter. Her lips had firmed, her chin set differently. Gilly ran her fingers through her hair and watched as the waves of hair fell back onto her straight, firm shoulders. *Goodness, I even stand differently!*

She smiled with just a touch of sadness. "Is this the Gilly Holmes you see, Joe? The one who *can't* let anyone take over her life, who fought so hard to stand tall? Is it, Joe . . . ?" Gilly closed her eyes and settled back in the chair, her mind playing gingerly with the confusing tapestry of her life.

She plucked a flower from the overflowing ceramic jug and breathed deeply, enjoying its fragrance. She looked exactingly around the room.

The dining room was as clean as it had ever been, or would ever be, she decided with a grin. Jars of pens and pencils were lined up on shelves and the drawing board was clean and empty. Pots of flowers were everywhere, and smells of Tugg's pizzas drifted in from the kitchen. She smiled, pleased with their afternoon of backbreaking, frantic work as she wandered through the kitchen and out onto the patio.

"Tugg, everything looks terrific!" Brushing a kiss across the tall man's cheek, Gilly slipped into the wide hammock that hung like a low cloud from the edge of the house to the one gnarled elm tree that shadowed the tiny back yard. "We did it!"

"Did you doubt it, madam?" Tugg's mouth twisted into a bearded grin. "Is there anything Holmes and Waters can't do?"

Gilly laughed. "No, I guess not. We are quite wonderful. And if the firm falls apart, we can always go into party planning."

Tugg groaned, then took a long, slow swig of his beer. "Sorry, partner. I'm afraid I've used up a lifetime's enthusiasm on this one event. And only for you would I do it!" Tugg straightened a Japanese lantern hanging gaily above him and headed for the back door. "Enough idle locution. I still have five pizzas to go, m'lady. And if you should see fit to get off your lovely tush, there's still one string of lanterns to hang." He nodded toward a colorful heap near the hedge. "By the way, Gilly, is Joe coming tonight?"

Gilly stopped the leap of her heart on its first flip. She was getting much better at it! "I think so," she answered nonchalantly. "We'll see."

Accepting her hedge Tugg strode back into the house, letting the screen door swing lazily shut behind him.

Was Joe coming? His reaction to the card certainly hadn't been what she'd expected. Her thoughts drifted back to his phone call, the sound of his voice filling the small patio.

"Gilly? At last! That damn answering phone of yours was beginning to drive me crazy." His voice had been low and rumbling with emotion.

"Hi, Joe! Sorry about the recording, but when Tugg and I are frantic about a deadline, it's a lifesaver." Rumbling or not it had been a welcome relief to hear his deep voice, a haven in the hectic week. "How are you?"

"Gilly, this invitation—"

"Oh, it got there. Good," Gilly had said softly.

"Why didn't you tell me sooner?"

"Well, I'm sorry, Joe, but the—"

"I could have arranged the party at the country club. A band, catered dinner. The whole works! You deserve it, Gilly. Your thirtieth birthday should be a gala!"

"Well"—she'd laughed—"I'm not sure of the gala part, but it *will* be fun. And I want everyone to meet you, Joe."

"And I want to meet your friends, Gilly. Now, I think I might still be able to swing the Philadelphia Club downtown. I called and—"

"Oh, Joe . . ." Gilly tried to hide the disappointment in her voice. He was being so thoughtful . . . and loving . . . and he didn't understand at all.

She forced a lightness into her voice. "No, Joe, you don't understand—this is *my* party. I'm having it here. At my house. Because I *want* it here."

"But it would be wonderful at the club. So much easier for you than the other way. And I'd like to do it for you, Gilly, to give a birthday party for you—"

Gilly's eyes had stung. He *hadn't* understood, didn't have the faintest idea what the party was all about. She swallowed her sadness and cleared her voice.

"Joe, wait." The strength of her voice had blanketed Joe's, coaxing it into silence. "Please, let's stop the talk of clubs and bands. It's all decided. It's here, and I want you to come." Her voice softened. "I want you here *very* much, Joe. Eight o'clock. I've got to go now."

Timmy and Henry had raced into the room just then, and Joe's good-bye was blurred. And it perfectly matched her thoughts, Gilly decided as she hung up the phone. Fuzzy. Sometimes she felt she and Joe were light-years apart in their minds, their thinking about life.

Gilly leaned back in the hammock and looked up into the endless depth of the darkening sky. Would Joe come? Her heart said yes. A single star appeared on the edge of her vision and blinked back at her. Gilly grinned and shut her eyes tightly. "Star light, star bright, first star I see tonight. I wish . . ." She chanted the childhood poem with a smile on her lips, a lighthearted feeling calming the tugging at her heart. Yes, Joe would come. . . .

"Gilly?" Tugg's voice boomed through the screen door. "I'm going home. Be back tonight. Don't touch one piece of pepperoni in here or I'll picket the party!" His voice drifted off with orders to shower and dress, and Gilly found herself tiredly following him into the house to catch a quick nap.

At precisely seven thirty-five the doorbell rang.

Gilly scrambled for a towel and raced to the bedroom door, leaving tiny puddles of water in her wake. "Timmy, would you please get the door?" Her words echoed back through the deserted house with the reminder that Timmy was spending the night at Adam's. She moaned and looked helplessly around the room. Grabbing a terry robe she pulled it tight, raced down the hall and to the door, and opened it.

"Gilly . . ."

Her heart hammered against her ribs. "Yes. In the flesh." Gilly blushed at her bad choice of words. Pressing one hand to her chest to calm herself, she took a step backward. "Please, Joe, come in." She clutched the bathrobe securely in one hand, pretended she looked presentable, and looked him directly in the eyes. "I'm so glad you could come, Joe."

Her eyes were bright and shining, her cheeks rosy from the steam of the shower, and Joe was glued to the doorway, enchanted. "I came a little early."

Gilly's light laughter floated around him. "Yes, I noticed!"

Joe swallowed a huge lump that had swelled in his throat. He was, for perhaps the first time in his life, befuddled. It wasn't being early. It was standing so deliciously close to Gilly Holmes and trying not to wipe away the tiny beads of water that sparkled like raindrops on her bare skin; it was suddenly wanting to scoop Gilly up in his arms, cast her robe to the wind, and carry her off to bed.

Joe cleared his throat and leaned his suited shoulders against the door frame in what he hoped was a very casual pose. "Is there, ah, something about this party that you neglected to tell me?"

Gilly laughed self-consciously. "Yes, Mr. Bennett. I neglected to tell you that none of my friends are ever on time for anything. And that's why you find me in such an awkward position."

"Awkward? I find you in an absolutely lovely position, Ms. Holmes. . . ." His eyes finally gave in to desire and slowly scanned the length of her, from the damp tendrils of her thick hair, to the gentle rise and fall of her breasts beneath the robe, across the graceful curve of her hips, and down to the puddle of water that outlined her bare feet.

Gilly shivered beneath his devouring look. "Joe, come in. I'd scold Timmy if he did that, left someone standing out on the porch, and here I'm doing it myself. . . ." Her voice drifted off as she pressed against the wall for Joe to pass, then closed the door behind him. His arm brushed against the thin robe as he moved into the tiny hall and Gilly felt the heat pass through her body, felt her breasts grow firm. "I, ah, I guess I had better get dressed, Joe."

Joe wet his lips in an absent gesture. Venus, that was it! The birth of Venus, a beautiful, naked goddess, stepping out of a shell. His eyes moved slowly over her again and paused at the robe's lapel. When she closed the door, her robe fell open a crack and the rosy flesh of her breast now peeked through. Joe's breath caught in his throat.

In the distance Gilly's light chatter continued. ". . . because if I don't get dressed soon, people will be arriving and—"

Joe forced himself to focus in on her words. "Get dressed?"

"Yes," she choked. Joe's look had been enough to melt ice. If she didn't get away soon, she'd have a lot of explaining to do to thirty-some people about to be walking in her door! And if she didn't get away right *now,* she might not at all. . . . "Yes, Joe. I think it's a good idea." She moved a few feet down the hall, then tossed back over her shoulder, "There's a washtub of beer out on the patio. Help yourself."

Before he could answer, Gilly fled down the hallway while escape was still a willful option. She didn't glance back, didn't trust herself to see the look of intense desire hazing Joe Bennett's wonderful black eyes.

And when she reappeared a short time later, her hair brushed to a coppery sheen and her willowy body dressed in gray slacks and a brilliant blue sweater, there were so many people crowded into her kitchen and tiny patio that she couldn't have seen it if she tried.

In fact, for several minutes she couldn't see Joe Bennett at all, so engulfed was she in birthday hugs and greetings. Her friends had turned out en masse, from Father "Fitz" Fitzgerald—who ran a soup kitchen in downtown Philadelphia—to clients, neighbors, and her bluejean-clad friends from art school.

"Tugg"—Gilly pulled herself away from a laughing group and cornered the chef, complete with lopsided white hat, near the stove—"have you seen Joe?"

"He's here somewhere. I introduced him around as best I could. I think Mrs. Lewandowski from down the street has the hots for him. She's already promised him one of her famous cherry pies," Tugg joked as he wiped his forehead and peered into the oven to check his pizza. "He's a brave fellow, Gilly—"

"Brave?"

"To tackle your motley group of friends. That takes guts." Tugg grinned teasingly. "I've decided I like him."

Gilly drew her brows together. "Of course you do. But I didn't realize he was on trial."

"Touchy, touchy, Ms. Holmes." Tugg tweaked her playfully on the cheek. "You realize what that means,

94

that unreasonable sensitivity to a dear friend's comments, don't you?"

Gilly paused for just a fraction of a second before jerking his chef's hat down over his bushy eyebrows. "No, I haven't the faintest idea what that means, Dr. Goodheart." Gilly spun on her heels and escaped the heat of the kitchen before Tugg read farther into her heart.

The patio was a sea of colors: brightly patterned cotton blouses and peasant skirts, faded denims and bright shirts, all lit by the flickering sway of the Japanese lanterns. Father Fitz had carted an old upright piano from the church in his pickup truck, and now sat in his glory on the patio, his handsome head thrown back as he sang, his remarkable fingers dancing over the keys like those of a nightclub pro. Portly Mrs. Lewandowski stood gaily at his side, tapping her brown Oxford shoe to the music.

Joe Bennett stood off to the edge of the patio and listened to the engaging strains of "Stardust," his eyes drifting over the laughing, happy groups of people. They seemed so young, Joe thought, even though some that passed by him munching Tugg's pizza and carrying plastic cups of beer were obviously far beyond him in years. It was their gaiety, their looseness, maybe, and the laughter that lit their faces.

He watched intently, intrigued and vaguely disturbed by the portrait of Gilly they offered. Her friends didn't really surprise him, although he wasn't sure what to expect. He simply hadn't given it much thought. He'd only thought of Gilly, Gilly in isolation, Gilly with him. Now there were all these connections to consider in sorting out the woman who was keeping him up at night. Taking a long, cold drink of beer, Joe half closed his eyes and let the music lull the confusion swirling around inside his well-ordered mind.

Gilly stood just outside the screen door, her eyes skirting the crowd. Where was Joe? Her heart sank to her toes. Perhaps he'd left; perhaps he'd decided Gilly Holmes's birthday party wasn't where he wanted to be at all. She strained to see around the group gathered at the piano. What was he wearing? A sport jacket and tie, that's right. A tie! Good Lord, he must have felt as out of place here as she had in his office.

"Gilly." The rumble was there again as the rich voice traveled on the night air, deep and sensuous. Gilly looked into the shadows just off the patio, and Joe's outline became visible. She threaded her way to his side.

"Joe, I'm so glad you're still here! I thought maybe you'd left." Instinctively Gilly slipped her hand into the soothing warmth beneath his arm.

"Left?" Joe looked down at her, his eyes deep and crinkling at the corners. "Why would I leave? I haven't even had a chance to kiss the birthday girl! I'd have done it earlier"—he ran a finger along her cheek—"but I was afraid we'd never make it to the party if I had."

Gilly smiled shyly, feeling a warm blush wash across her cheeks. "Yes, well, we made it, didn't we?" She looked up into his startling black eyes. "And in perfect control."

Joe crooked one finger beneath her chin and tilted her head up until he could see the moonlight reflected in her eyes. "Control, Gilly? Hmmm . . ." His lips drew closer and his breath was a soft, warm breeze caressing her cheeks. "Yes, I'd say we're in perfect control. . . ."

In the space of a heartbeat his lips were claiming hers. Gilly's arms folded automatically around his neck, her fingers digging into the thick black hair above the nape of his neck as she returned his kiss.

"Mr. Bennett . . ."

Joe opened one eye, his lips still clinging to Gilly's, and looked down into the shadows. The gravelly voice belonged to a portly figure tapping him gently on the shoulder.

96

Gilly pulled away, her hand sliding down his back, then dropping to her side. She turned and looked.

The woman giggled. "Tsk, you two. Caught you!"

"Mrs. Lewandowski!" Gilly's throaty laugh lifted on a breeze.

"I was looking for your young man, Gilly. We need to become better acquainted, and I promised I'd teach him how to fox-trot." She grinned up at Joe and took his arm. "You can have him back later."

Gilly stared. Fox-trot? Joe? Joe caught her eye and winked. "Mrs. Lewandowski says fox-trotting helps the metabolism."

Gilly shook her head as the two walked off, watching them until they disappeared into the group. Her heart swelled. Joe's tall, strong body towered over her seventy-year-old neighbor's square form, his arm kindly guiding her wherever she wanted to go. She could see his dark head bend to catch a word or two, his husky laughter blend with the noisy festivities as Mrs. Lewandowski chatted on and on, probably about her seven cats, her cherry trees, and her one son who lived far away.

Squelching the desire to follow him and wrap her arms around his waist, Gilly mingled, playing the role of hostess with happy finesse. Joe's kiss stayed with her, warm on her lips, lighting her eyes.

"You look happy, kid. Must be my pizza," Tugg teased as he came up behind Gilly.

Gilly planted a kiss on his forehead. "That's for noticing."

"Noticing? Had I known ahead of time what you'd be like tonight, I would have pitched the Japanese lanterns. You're glowing brighter than the whole shebang!"

Gilly elbowed him in the side. "Enough, already."

"Enough? Never! The party's just beginning, my friend." And with that Tugg strode to the center of the patio, waving his hands to command attention while Fa-

97

ther Fitz assisted with a dramatic drum-roll on the piano. "Gather round and find yourselves a seat, folks. It's P-R-E-S-E-N-T time, as in thirtieth—can you buh-lieve it!—birthday!"

"Oh, Tugg," Gilly groaned as she slipped down on the patio bench. She scanned the crowd until she found Joe, who was surrounded by a group of art students who seemed to be hanging on his every word. She caught his eye and he threaded his way over to her, dropping down next to her on the bench.

Gilly tried to ignore the closeness of Joe and concentrated on Tugg as he joked his way through the spotlight. As Father Fitz filled in the background with crazy impromptu melodies, the presents were handed to Gilly and unwrapped: three hand-made pots, a lovely watercolor; a tiny silver dove on a chain made by a friend from school; one of Mrs. Lewandowski's cherry pies that dripped deliciously all over Joe's slacks; a framed photograph taken by Tugg of a joyfully triumphant Timmy making his first soccer goal; a cross-stitched sampler lovingly done by another of Gilly's elderly neighbors.

Joe's brows drew together unconsciously, his fingers tightening around a tiny box in his jacket pocket. He'd brought a present too. A lovely present, carefully, lovingly chosen. It matched Gilly's eyes: a deep azure blue. He pulled it out and looked down at the carefully wrapped square box. It matched her eyes, but didn't match anything else on the patio. Not the other gifts, not the warm, jovial mood, not Gilly . . .

Just as he fumbled for the pocket flap, Gilly looked over at him. Her eyes rested on the box and she smiled softly. "Joe, you didn't have to bring anything."

Joe stuffed the box back into his pocket. What was going on here? He felt suddenly unsure, hesitant, and anger rose up to fight the feeling. "It's nothing!" he said, stuffing the gift back inside the folds of his jacket. "Nothing at all."

"Joe?" Gilly sought his face for some explanation of his odd behavior. He offered none.

"Joe, what's the matter?"

"Nothing, Gilly. Oh, hell, here!" He jerked the box out and thrust it into her hands. Father Fitz had resumed his piano playing and the crowd began singing old Simon and Garfunkel tunes and no one noticed the vulnerable look on the handsome man's face as Gilly opened and held to the light a perfect star sapphire, hung on a delicate gold chain.

It was the most gorgeous gem she'd ever seen. The flickering light from the Japanese lantern sparkled off its surface, highlighting the star.

"Oh, Joe," she breathed, more to herself than to the man sitting uncomfortably next to her. "Oh, Joe, it's lovely. It's absolutely beautiful." She knew she shouldn't keep it, knew it probably cost as much as Holmes and Waters made in a month. But when she looked over into Joe's ebony eyes, her heart stopped.

"It's not a handmade pot, or a pie. . . ." His voice was low and husky. "But it *is* personal, Gilly. I tore this town apart until I found the exact color to match your eyes." Joe took the chain from her hand and held it next to her face, the cool jewel touching her cheek. "I was right. It's perfect." As assurance returned, he slipped it around her neck and shut the clasp.

Gilly dipped her chin to her chest and looked at the lovely round gem. Her voice caught in her throat and she fought against the tears gathering in the corners of her eyes. *It's this party . . . these dear people. . . .* she whispered silently. *Everything is starting to get to me . . . must come with turning thirty. . . .* Slowly she raised her head and fell into Joe's waiting look. "It's a wonderful birthday gift. Thank you, Joe. . . ." Then, forcing a lightness into her voice and a grin across her lips, she rose from the bench, pulling Joe up after her.

"Now, how would you like to dance with the birthday girl? I hear you do a mean fox-trot."

Joe grinned, wrapped his arm firmly around her waist, and swept her lightly over the uneven patio stones and into the night. "Happy birthday, Gillian Holmes," he murmured into her ear, then pulled her closer, letting nothing come between them.

"It's been a great party, Gilly!" The screen door slammed shut as Tugg sauntered into the kitchen. "You turn old with real pizzazz, my friend."

Gilly laughed wearily as she slumped down in a kitchen chair. "Thanks a heap, Tugg." She looked out the screen door just in time to see Joe help Mrs. Lewandowski around the corner of the house.

Tugg followed her look. "Joe's a real trouper, you know? I have a sneaking suspicion he doesn't go to many pizza parties, but he tried his darndest to fit in . . . and everyone loved him, Gilly. Even though he wasn't on trial here or anything!" Tugg's eyes twinkled teasingly as he grabbed some detergent from beneath the counter. "And while I'm speaking my mind, kiddo, he's lit something in you that sure is nice to see. Hope you don't go and blow it out now."

Gilly leaned her head back and closed her eyes briefly. Tugg knew her so well. He knew how hard it had been during those years of school and he knew her fierce fight for self-confidence. He also knew she'd set aside any "involving" relationships to work on herself, to feel intact and good about herself. But Joe had slipped in anyway . . . and Tugg was right. She sure didn't want to "blow out" the wonderful way he made her feel either! "I like him very much, Tugg."

"And?"

Gilly paused for a minute, then shook her head, rose, and headed for the sink. *"And . . .* Tugg-o, if we don't get these dishes started soon, you're going to sadly disappoint Jayne with the punk hairdo who happens to be sitting out in your Jeep with passion dripping from her false eyelashes!"

"Ah, Jayne. Yes." Tugg eagerly grabbed for a towel as he looked out on the deserted backyard. "You really should have accepted some of those offers to help clean up, Gilly!"

Gilly grinned and patted soapsuds on his arm. "Patience, my dear." She glanced outside before dipping her hands back into the water. "It *is* empty out there, isn't it? Has everyone gone?"

"I think so. Joe and Mrs. L were the last to leave."

Joe. Gilly peered through the window into the darkness. She'd thought he was just walking her elderly neighbor home, then would be back. But she only lived two doors down. He should be back by now. If he was coming back . . .

"Scrub, Gilly, scrub," Tugg slipped a handful of dirty silverware into the sink urging her back to work.

"Sure, Tugg," she murmured softly, filled inexplicably with a sad longing.

Joe slipped soundlessly through the front door a short while later, then walked back toward the voices coming from the kitchen. Gilly and Tugg were standing at the sink, their backs to him. He leaned against the door frame for a minute, watching them as they piled up clean dishes and mugs.

Gilly was laughing now at something Tugg had said, her head tilted back slightly and her thick, silky hair grazing the gentle arch of her back. Her blue sweater outlined the curve of her breasts, and Joe watched them rise and fall slowly. His mind's eye slipped back to Gilly

101

standing in the front hallway hours before, water dripping from the curves of her body, her hair a tangle of wet waves as she stood shivering beneath the robe. God, she was lovely. His chest heaved beneath the starched fabric of his shirt.

"You going to clean all this tonight?" His voice filled the room, deep and resonant, sending Gilly spinning clear around.

"Joe!" Her hands flew to her cheeks as soapsuds scattered through the air, collecting like snowflakes on Tugg's beard.

"Sorry to frighten you." His black eyes caressed her face.

"No, no." Her breath was ragged. She was so glad to see him, so glad he hadn't gone home! "Where were you?"

"Took Ida Lewandowski home." His eyes stayed glued to her face. "Great lady. She wanted me to come in and meet Harrison, her parakeet. He used to belong to a sailor, but I really think it's Ida who's taught him most of his bawdy repertoire."

Gilly watched the tiny laugh lines fan out from his magical eyes.

"Looks like you two got stuck with KP." His eyes skirted over the sink of dirty dishes to the littered patio beyond.

"Yeah." Tugg laughed as he turned back and picked up a dish. "It's a darn shame the maid took the night off."

Joe looked around. He didn't know a damn thing about cleaning up a kitchen. He'd have offered to send his maid over in the morning but had a feeling *that* idea would fly like a lead balloon. But one thing he knew for sure. He wasn't leaving Gilly's house.

Shrugging out of his jacket he tossed it over the back of a kitchen chair and stepped up, putting his arms casually around Gilly's waist.

102

"Well, anyone can dry a dish, right?"

Before either Gilly or Tugg could speak, Joe took the towel that slipped readily from Tugg's hand.

"Tugg, my friend, you have a damsel wrapped around your steering wheel waiting anxiously for you. I'll take over here." He caught and held Gilly in the swirling black depths of his eyes. "Gilly and I can manage just fine. . . ."

CHAPTER SEVEN

"I thought you'd never offer!" With a grin that said he wondered why it had taken Joe so long, the bearded photographer was out the door, stopping only long enough to drop a kiss on the top of Gilly's head.

Gilly stood still at the sink, her eyes never leaving Joe's face.

Submerging his hand into the dishwater Joe pulled the plug out with a muffled pop and dropped it onto the side of the sink.

"Joe, what about the dishes?"

"Don't worry, Gilly," he spoke softly into her hair. Picking the dishtowel up from the counter Joe pulled her hands from the sink and dried them gently between the terry folds of material.

Gilly's eyes traveled up to his face. "Joe, it's the dishes that need drying, not me." But her hands remained between his, absorbing the wonderful warm feel of his fingers as they rubbed against her own.

"No one should have to clean up after her own birthday party, Gilly. It's bad luck." The dishtowel slipped forgotten to the floor as Joe led her into the darkened living room.

Stray moonbeams fell through the sashed curtains and lined the golden floor in wavy stripes. As she stepped noiselessly through them, Gilly felt the tiredness easing out of her body, replaced almost instantly by a new, delicious tension. She slipped down onto the couch and welcomed the feel of solidness beneath her.

Joe stretched his long body down beside hers. "There. Now, relax, Gilly. It's been a long day for you."

Gilly glanced over at his moonlit shape, nodding in agreement. "And it's not nearly over. You're a bad influence on me, Joe. I don't sleep well if I know I'll be waking up to a mess in my kitchen. We'll relax for just a moment, then back to the salt mines." She burrowed into the couch as she spoke, her lean body curling into a comfortable position, her feet slipping out of her shoes and up beneath her.

She felt Joe's smile in the darkened room. The guardedness she sometimes saw in Joe hadn't been there all night, she mused silently. Nice. Very nice. Gilly welcomed the feel of his arm as it wrapped around the back of the couch, cradling her neck in its bend. "Mmmm."

"I agree." Joe pulled her closer until the warmth of her body completely blotted out the edges of autumn chill. She fit so perfectly in his arms. "Gilly," he whispered, one hand resting as gently as a butterfly on her thigh, the other slowly caressing her cheek with the broad, smooth side of his thumb, "happy birthday. . . ."

Gilly felt a feverish rush flow through her. His hand was burning its imprint on her thigh. She shifted slightly on the couch but was unable and unwilling to pull herself away from the exciting warmth of his arms. "Thank you,

Joe," she murmured softly. "Getting older isn't such a bad thing. I don't know why people are afraid of it."

Joe moved his head until his lips almost touched her cheek. "Nope, it's not such a bad thing at all. And I have a feeling it'll get better and better and better. . . ." His breath warmed her cheek, sending rivers of pleasure flowing through her.

His fingers were gently moving along the sensitive skin of her thigh, and Gilly found breathing took major effort. "Joe, it's nearly dish time, I think. . . ." Her words were hushed and meaningless and coaxed a slow smile to Joe's lips.

"Gilly, I haven't dried a dish since I was eleven years old, and I don't intend to start tonight." He kissed her slowly and lovingly until he felt her lips relax beneath his own. Pulling back just enough to look into her eyes, he spoke again. "My beautiful Gilly, the only thing in the universe I want to do tonight is to love you. Gilly, I want you so very much. . . ."

Jaggedly she forced air into her lungs. "You don't beat around the bush, do you?"

"You want it, too, Gilly. I can see it in your eyes. That wonderful luster . . ." His hand pressed more firmly on her thigh, igniting each nerve ending beneath the soft gray wool of her slacks.

Gilly turned her head until the cool air beyond Joe's body soothed her flushed cheeks and neck. Then, tucking her head beneath his chest, she nuzzled closely to him. Oh, yes, she wanted him! Wanted him so very much.

Joe's hand stroked her cheek gently, and the other moved slowly up her rib cage until it came to rest just beneath her breasts, stopping her breath in her throat. His thumb rubbed slowly against the firm curve, then moved in slow circles until Gilly felt her breasts grow firm and tingly.

"Oh, Joe." She gasped, feeling her body fill with liquid fire.

"Gilly, my Gilly," he murmured softly into her hair as his lips sought, then found, the smooth skin of her forehead, dropping tiny kisses along its breadth. His lips dropped to the tip of her ear, then nuzzled into the sweet hollow of her throat. "My darling Gilly."

Gilly's hand found its way into the thick mass of wavy hair above his neck just an instant before his lips rose to claim her own. Every ounce of logical reserve dissolved in the space of a heartbeat as she melted willingly into his embrace. Angling her body Gilly deepened the kiss.

It was Joe who first came up for air. "You sure do know how to kiss, Gilly Holmes," he breathed with difficulty.

"It must come with turning thirty," she murmured. "A birthday kiss . . ." She felt abandonment wash over her like a soothing salve, felt the hot rush of desire fan out from the core of her and lift her into wonderland.

His hand had slipped beneath the softness of her sweater and moved with gentle strides over her midriff until stopped by the rise of her breasts. Slowly he slipped his fingers beneath the wisp of filmy lingerie and surrounded the silky skin of her breast. It was smooth and warm. Deliciously warm, just as he knew it would be. Gilly's body pressed closer and Joe felt himself grow hot beneath her.

"Gilly . . ." He pressed himself into the back of the small sofa for a moment to regain some control, then moved his hands to her shoulders and looked into her eyes. She was beautiful and passionate, and unlike any woman he'd ever known before. He wanted her—totally —heart and soul and body. He wanted *all* of Gilly Holmes.

She met his look with a smile that seared his soul and took away any need for words.

Joe rose from the couch, bent his dark, tousled head to her chest, and scooped her up in his arms. "Down the hall?" he murmured into the honey fall of hair that caressed his cheek.

Gilly wound her arms around his neck and nodded.

He found it easily, guided by his heartbeat and the lovely woman cradled in his arms.

Joe walked slowly over to the four-poster bed and set Gilly down into the soft cushion of the patchwork quilt like a porcelain doll.

She lay still, gazing into Joe's eyes. His face was tender, stripped of the defenses that were such a part of him. The strength that lined his jaw was still there, but tempered with gentleness and longing. Gilly reached up slowly and touched the skin roughened by a day's growth of beard. Her eyes, cloudy with need, urged him forward. "Joe," she whispered, a touch of laughter lightening her tone, "would you like to take off your tie?"

In one smooth sweep the neatly striped tie lay coiled like a snake on the braided rug beneath him. "Thank you, ma'am," he whispered roughly, his words thick with desire. "And now may I sit down?"

Twining her fingers through his Gilly drew him to her bed. He pressed his long body against hers, one elbow angled beneath him so he could see her face. His knee eased its way between her legs. "You know, Gilly," he said, his hand roaming up and down the fuzzy sweater, then slipping beneath, "it's much too hot in here for this. May I?" And without waiting for an answer he coaxed her arms above her head and slipped the sweater off in a clean sweep. Next came the lacy camisole, followed by a husky groan as his eyes focused on her soft perfect breasts splashed with golden moonlight. The star sapphire rested just between them.

Joe's whole body tightened in response to her. In a mindless movement he kicked off his shoes and slipped

108

his pants down and over the end of the bed. He fumbled with the buttons on his shirt until Gilly lazily reached out and helped.

Joe felt the world fall away. All that was real was the torrent of emotion he felt for Gilly, the thrilling anticipation of her, the surge of desire that throbbed in every part of him.

Gilly's fingers ran over his chest, rubbing his hair between her fingers, then pressing her palms into the hard, rough skin. She wanted to feel every inch of him, to know the broadness of his chest through her fingers, to feel his heartbeat pounding into her palm. She wanted more than anything in the world to be pressed so closely to Joe Bennett that not even the tiniest atom could come between them. It was almost painful, Gilly thought fleetingly—painful and so wonderfully joyous she could barely breathe. She twisted, her hips beginning to move slowly against him.

Joe's fingers ran over her breasts, then slid down her smooth skin toward the waistband of her slacks. Releasing the catch, his fingers felt beneath the material, spreading over the firm skin of her abdomen, then dipping lower until Gilly felt the earth spin beneath her. There was no fear, no hesitation, no doubt, only an incredible heated desire to be loved by this man, and no one else. Shaking, she helped him remove the last of her clothing, then lay back and cradled his head to her breasts.

Joe caressed them eagerly, taking first one, then the other, into his mouth. The sweet taste of her spun inside his head until he was dizzy. "Gilly, you're doing incredible things to me. . . ."

"*You*'re incredible, Joe. . . ." Her hands wound around him, charting the span of muscles on his hard back, kneading them, committing to memory every slight movement of him beneath her touch.

Pulling aside slightly Joe gazed dreamily down into her eyes. "Gilly, I've thought of this moment since that day at the campsite—"

"When you led us blindly along the wrong trail," she teased in a whisper.

His fingers moved down her belly, burning trails into the creamy skin. "Never again will I take the wrong trail," he said huskily, his hands now burning into her thighs. "Never, Gilly."

Gilly gasped as she grew warm and moist. "Oh, Joe, I want you so." *More than logic or the pattern of my life allows. I want you, Joe Bennett. . . .*

Gently he rolled on top of her, his hands cradling her shoulders, his breath a passionate whisper in her hair. Her hands wound tightly around his neck as he slowly came into her, surely and gently, with care he hadn't known he possessed. He moved slowly until he felt her respond in sensuous rhythm, her body dancing with his own, her thighs pressing around him firmly and tightly. He wanted to soar with her, so high above the clouds that the world would be a tiny speck of nothing, heaven their only base.

"Gilly, Gilly," he whispered as he smothered her face in kisses.

Her name dropped like kisses from his lips, and Gilly felt all thought leave her. All she felt was the incredible explosive joy of spinning away from the earth. A blinding flash of fire went through her, followed immediately by a sea of incredible warmth that carried her to heaven on a cloud of love. Their sighs fused together as they fell to earth cushioned in one another's arms.

Thin strands of light pulled Joe awake. His body fought it at first, and he burrowed deeper into the tousled sheets. Then morning sounds reached his ears and he opened one eye. It was Saturday. The day of the week

110

was the first thing Joe always thought of. Followed by an instinctive reflex to turn on the radio and get the weather report and news. But today was different.

He reached across the bed instead, a slow, contented smile softening his face. Gilly.

His body turned as his fingers groped for the now-familiar softness of her body. Instead they settled around an empty, cold pillow. Joe sat up and looked around. He was alone.

So this was Gilly's bedroom. His eyes traveled over the clean tasteful furnishings. It was an artist's room, lovely and simple, like Gilly. The kind of simple that looked that way only because someone put great care and attention to it.

The color in the room came from several large paintings positioned against the white walls. One was a vibrant splash of warm tones that defined nothing, but was very pleasing to the eye. Joe smiled. The colors were a swirl of warmth that perfectly matched the way he felt. He'd never liked abstract art before—but perhaps it was time for a change.

The furniture in Gilly's room was simple oak, probably inherited from a grandmother, he decided, and polished lovingly to a shine that brought out each wavy grain of the wood. White filmy curtains blew in the slightly open window, casting shadows across the bed. It was perfect.

The floor was warm hardwood, its expanse broken only by the thick braided rug beside the bed. That he remembered from the night. He'd felt the gentle roll of braid beneath his feet when he'd crept out of the room before dawn to retrieve the vintage bottle of champagne he'd brought Gilly for her birthday. He'd awakened Gilly gently and they'd sat naked together in the middle of the quilted bed in the darkest moments of night, toasting the night and day, life, and each other. They'd laughed freely

111

and openly, shared intimacies, and fallen naturally into each other's arms in a swirl of lovemaking.

A slow smile curled his lips as Joe fell back into the pillows, his eyes half closed, his body and soul enjoying each ripe moment of memory.

Gilly stood quietly in the doorway watching him. His dark hair was tousled against the stark white pillowcase, his broad, bare chest gleaming in the sunshine. She followed the line of his body from his strong-set jaw, over his broad shoulders, down over the expanse of chest to the flatness of his abdomen as it disappeared beneath the sheet. It took less than imagination to follow what the thin white material attempted to cover, and Gilly felt her knees melt into Jell-O as she stared unabashedly at the outline. "Joe," she whispered unthinking.

A slow smile that started in his dark eyes and spread outward greeted her. His eyes slowly opened and focused on the silhouette in the doorway. She had on a pair of faded jeans and a bulky emerald-green sweater, her cinnamon-dusted hair loose and shining about her shoulders. She smiled softly, and Joe watched the words form on her lips still fresh from his kisses.

"Good morning, sleepyhead."

"I was drugged." His smile swallowed her.

"Me too."

"Come here. . . ." Joe held his arms out, the sheet slipping lower.

Gilly felt the familiar rush of desire sweep through her and leaned against the cool door frame for support. "I can't."

"Feet glued to the floor? I'd be happy to unglue you." Joe leaned forward, his eyes mischievous.

"You already have, Joe," she answered huskily. "Would you like a cup of coffee?"

"I'd like *you.*"

Gilly's look caressed his face, memorized the look of

ove and wanting there, knew she mirrored it as clearly as trees in a still, glassy lake. "It's Saturday, Joe. I promised Tim we'd go to the park." The words sounded tinny when they reached her ears. Tinny and unreal. Saturday, Sunday, Tuesday. Joe had pulled the days out from beneath her and thrown them away. He had stopped time. She took a deep breath and stood straight, her shoulders squared back. Joe's rumbling laugh circled the room.

"You look like you're squaring off for battle, Gilly my love. What's wrong?"

Gilly dissolved in laughter, her shoulders dipping forward, her head moving from side to side. "You, that's what, Joe Bennett!"

"What have I done?"

"Thrown me a curve ball!" She looked up at him from beneath a thick fringe of lashes. "And I'm a terrible catcher. Ask Timmy."

"I'll teach you, Gilly. Don't worry."

His eyes swallowed her, and Gilly looked at him with longing. She didn't want day to intrude. But it had to. "Joe, coffee's ready. And eggs and bacon and a cherry pie."

"Cherry pie?"

"Yep. I went out early to ride my bike to see if I could still breathe." She grinned. "I could . . . a little . . . with extreme difficulty. Anyway, Mrs. Lewandowski was feeding the cats and waiting for me." She brushed a strand of hair behind one ear, her head tilting to one side.

"Ah, let me guess. My car—"

"Right! Your car parked at my curb brought her great delight. I haven't seen her eyes sparkle that brightly since Timmy gave her his biggest Valentine last year. She was grinning from ear to ear! Without saying a word, but with a look that would make *you* blush, she rushed down the steps, piled my bike basket with homemade muffins and a cherry pie, and kissed me on the cheek. 'In case you have company for breakfast,' she whispered mysteriously, then ran back inside."

Joe laughed gustily. "I knew Ida would stand by me! It was written all over her. 'Love me, love my parakeet, and I'll be your friend forever!' "

"Well, she'll be terribly hurt if she comes over and finds that pie uneaten. And since she just might 'drop in' any minute, and since I need to collect Timmy and fly to a soccer game, you had better make yourself decent, Mr. Bennett. Pronto!"

Joe groaned. "You mean we can't . . ."

Gilly blushed. "That's what I mean."

Joe sat upright and swung his long legs lazily over the side of the bed. "Well, my lovely Gilly, it's your house, your rules. . . ." His dark eyes flashed and held her still in the doorway. "You may be able to take Joe out of the love bed . . . but you can't take the love out of Joe." In several swift movements he was towering over her, his pants pulled on carelessly and hanging loosely on his hips, his lips pressed into her hair, his arms holding her close. "We Bennetts are very difficult to get rid of once we attach ourselves. I'll be here, Gilly. I'll take care of you. You'll see, Gilly, you'll see. . . ."

CHAPTER EIGHT

"Bet you'd have more fun with Joe."

"Of course I would." Gilly smoothed down the simple black dress as she checked herself in the mirror.

"And he asked you out tonight, right?" Timmy flopped down on the floor and watched Gilly's reflection in the mirror.

"Right."

"Was he mad you said no?"

"I don't know, Timmy." Mad? Maybe a little. Upset for sure. Joe would have them together every minute—not that the thought wasn't appealing—but there were things Gilly couldn't, and wouldn't, let slide. Like her hostessing job at the Papillon. Besides, she needed the money, a subject, she learned quickly, that should never be brought up with Joe. So tonight *he'd* have to settle for taking clients out, and *she'd* go to work. Tomorrow—Gilly's cheeks glowed in anticipation—tomorrow they'd bundle up in heavy sweaters and would spend the whole day together, taking Mary and the kids on a leaf-finding trip through the brilliantly painted woods and fields of Bucks County.

The roller-coaster ride she and Joe had been on the past few weeks was incredibly wonderful. They had moved together through the brilliant haze of autumn, feeling the snap of life around them, inside of them, sweeping them up in a glow that was all their own. Gilly couldn't remember ever having been so happy!

"He really likes us, Mom." Timmy tossed a ball across the bedroom and Henry lumbered after it.

Gilly looked down at Tim's tousled head and grinned. "Sure he does, Tim. We're nice guys, don't you think?"

"Yeah. But he likes us more than nice. Adam says so too. And you know what Gram Bennett says?"

Gilly pulled her black wool coat from the closet and frowned at the signs of wear around the cuffs.

"*Gram* Bennett?" She raised one brow.

"Yeah, that's what all the kids call her."

"Oh." Gilly smiled softly. Gram Bennett. And Gram she was, the dearest friend and supporter those kids could ever have. Timmy worshiped her, and being around her was good for him, Gilly knew, good to have an older adult's influence at times. A *wiser* adult's. Heaven knew her head wasn't always as clear as it should be these days! "Just what does Gram Bennett say, Timmy?"

"Adam heard her tell that crabby cook who doesn't like Henry that we're the best medicine for Joe she could have found *anywhere,* that's what." Timmy's chest puffed out proudly. It deflated slightly as he added with a frown, "He musta been sick."

Gilly ruffled Tim's hair and said softly, "I guess so." Timmy never asked direct questions about her and Joe, and neither did Adam. For now, Gilly found relief in that, even though Adam had long ago wormed his way

116

right into her heart, and she knew Timmy and Joe were very fond of each other. The two little boys were like little stage prompters, always there, always quietly watching, always happy to push their parents out the door while they cornered Mary for a heated game of kid trivia. Their cupid attacks were subtle, but real.

Timmy caught his mother's amused smile and pulled his brows together. "What did I do?"

"Nothing." She leaned over and kissed him on the head.

Timmy caught her eye. "That's your mushy smile, Mom. Don't go mushy on me." His blue eyes sparkled mischievously. "Save that for Joe."

"Hey." Gilly crouched down and looked at him eye to eye. "You're not getting out of this so easily, my man. You are, and always will be, my number-one target for mushy smiles. There's no getting out of it. Sorry."

Timmy let one shoulder droop and hugged her tightly. "Aw, Mom!"

"Now, kiddo"—Gilly stood, her eyes still soft and moist—"I think I hear Tugg rummaging around in the refrigerator. Why don't you make him one of your super-duper peanut-butter–mayonnaise–cream-cheese sandwiches before you help him develop that film?" She kissed him lovingly on the top of his bobbing head, pointing him and Henry toward the kitchen, and moved out the door, her heart feeling mushier than her smile.

Gilly spoke pleasantly to the young couple as she seated them at an intimate corner table. Wishing them a nice evening she walked smoothly back across the carpeted room, pausing to straighten a tiny wrinkle in a rose-colored tablecloth, then to thank an elderly gentleman who offered her compliments on her tasteful black dress and the single star sapphire that lay elegantly on its yoke.

117

Picking up two gold-edged menus she positioned herself near the door.

"Ah, Gillian, a fine evening for Papillon's!" The tuxedoed owner brushed an ash-colored wisp of hair back in place as his smile beamed around the beautifully appointed restaurant.

"As usual, Gordon!" Gilly laughed as she followed his proud perusal of the business into which he'd poured his heart and soul and lifetime savings.

It was a lovely restaurant, from the fine food and the fresh-cut roses in slender vases to the long-gowned harpist seated gracefully beneath the carefully chosen Impressionist paintings. And it had earned Gordon a well-deserved four-star rating by Philadelphia food critics.

Gilly liked the sixty-year-old owner and was happy for him. Even though working part time at Papillon's was tiring, especially after a full day in the studio, she liked *that,* too. There was something almost refreshing about it, something so different from the world of layouts and prints, that she felt it almost an emotional necessity. Much cheaper than therapy, she'd laughingly told Tugg earlier that night. "Gordon, I think the new menu for winter looks terrific. Business will be better than ever."

"Ah, Gillian, what would you say if I asked you to become a permanent hostess here in our little bit of heaven?" Gordon teased, pleased by her praise.

"Probably exactly what I said last time you asked me, Gordon." Gilly laughed. *"Only* if you promise to give me your secret, prize-winning recipe for veal mistral à la Gordon. I'd *die* for that!" She growled.

"Och, women!" Gordon moaned dramatically, clasping the sides of his head. "Always wanting the impossible!" And then he sobered quickly to greet a group of arriving patrons.

The first hour passed quickly. Gilly checked on the waitresses, answered questions, smiled warmly, as she glided back and forth across the restaurant keeping everyone happy and things running smoothly. And they *did* run smoothly. Until a few minutes after nine o'clock when her heart skipped a beat and her breath collected in an immovable lump right in the middle of her throat.

He stood over near the reservation desk, bigger than life, and even more ruggedly handsome than usual. Joe Bennett and his three gentlemen companions were standing in the doorway, chatting with Gordon and obviously waiting for a table.

"Gilly, you okay?" One of the waitresses stopped short at the sight of the always-composed Gilly, standing stockstill in the kitchen doorway, her arms raised in thin air, staring across the room.

Gilly let out her breath. "Oh. Oh, sure, Rita. I'm just fine. Great!" She flashed her a brilliant smile and hurried across the room. Joe! What a wonderful surprise!

He didn't see her for a minute, saw only a flash of black as a small figure walked up beside the group. It wasn't until her hand rested lightly on his arm that Joe looked at her. And it wasn't until she said, "Joe, I'm so glad to see you!" and set down the stack of menus she held in her hands that he lost his cool.

In a fraction of a second the pleasant smile was wiped from his face and his brows drew together in a harsh stare. "Gilly! What are you doing here?"

Gilly took a startled step backward.

The three men with him looked first at Joe, then at Gilly, then directed their uncomfortable glances toward Gordon.

"Gillian." Gordon spoke quickly, confused at the look on Joe Bennett's face. Joe was a good customer. Why was he so angry? "You know Mr. Bennett?"

"Yes.. Yes, I do, Gordon." She smiled brightly at Joe. What in heaven's name was the matter with him? "Joe, I had no idea this is where you'd be bringing your clients."

119

She turned toward the men, smiled warmly at Gordon, and looked back to Joe. "But it does confirm what good taste you have."

Joe swallowed hard, trying to block out the anger that was threatening to choke him. "What are you doing here? You said you had to work tonight." His voice was low and controlled.

"Yes. I work here. Whenever Gordon needs a hostess to fill in."

"She's the very best, Mr. Bennett. I try to talk her into full time, but she turns me down every time."

Joe forced a smile, then managed polite introductions to his out-of-town clients. "Gordon, would you mind seating my friends? I'd like to talk to Gilly for a moment."

"Certainly, Mr. Bennett." He bowed slightly and led the gentlemen away.

"What do you mean, you work here?" Joe demanded as soon as the men were out of earshot.

Gilly felt her muscles tighten. Felt her back stiffen as she tried to make sense out of his anger. Her breath caught in her throat as he loomed before her, bigger than life, like a restrained wild stallion.

"Joe, what's the matter? I work here part time, and have for nearly a year and a half. It's a nice extra job that helps pay the bills." She forced a smile to her lips.

"But why, Gilly?" he demanded, his eyes flashing fire. "You already have a job that takes up too much of your time! Now another? And you never as much as mentioned it to me?"

Gilly clenched her fists tightly at her sides and forced her words out in low, even tones. "Joe, we've been through all this before. My business is still getting on its feet. This job is great because it helps me buy extra equipment so we'll grow faster, and I never mentioned it because there was no need to, Joe." Her eyes pleaded with him to understand, but Joe was silent. "I support Timmy and myself in the best way I know how, can't you see that?"

Joe didn't speak, but the set of his head, the clenched muscles in his jaw, took the place of words. Joe didn't understand. "Joe"—Gilly raised her head and spoke directly—"Joe, I don't understand why this has you so upset, but I'm afraid I don't have the time right now to stay around and find out. I have work to do."

Before he could respond, she spun on her heels, picked up the stack of menus, and hurried off to seat a party of four waiting patiently for their table. Slowly Joe walked back to his table, his broad shoulders tense beneath the wool tweed jacket.

The others were engaged in an animated discussion on a new microcomputer and Joe sat down quietly, forcing himself back into the role of host. His eyes moved from one man to the next, a smile curving his lips now and then, a frown when the tone became serious.

But Joe Bennett didn't hear a word. All his thoughts were centered on the woman moving graciously from table to table, seating people, her soft, warm smile charming everyone. His Gilly, the woman he loved.

His eyes followed her, recording every movement. Yes, he *did* love Gilly. It filled him, easing a pain he'd lived with for so long, as it spread like soothing salve into ragged wounds. Excited him. But tonight he wasn't feeling the soothing warmth or the excitement; tonight Joe Bennett felt a cutting, relentless anger.

Why had she kept this secret from him? She shouldn't be working here on top of everything else she did. And she didn't need to. Hell, she knew that! Knew he'd take care of anything for her. He'd change the color of the moon if it would ease her life! Then why—why?—hadn't she come to him to help her? His stomach tightened as he

121

followed Gilly's movements, trying fiercely to understand.

"Joe?" The deep, laughing voice of Ed Piebenga, his client and an old friend from Pittsburgh, scattered his thoughts.

Joe looked up quickly. "Yes, Ed?"

"Just wondered if that's a Philadelphia custom?"

"What?"

"The pear in your fruit salad. You've been cutting it with your knife for five minutes."

Joe stared at his plate, then jerked his eyes back to Ed's. Control drifted back as he muted his feelings with laughter. "As a matter of fact, it is. Proven fact that it aids digestion. The news should reach Pittsburgh in a few years or so."

The men laughed and followed up with easy banter that drew Joe back into their midst.

From a few tables away Gilly saw the crinkles appear at the corners of his eyes, then the laughter that followed, and she slowly released the breath she'd been holding for an eternity. There, he looked like Joe again. Smiling, his black eyes deep and warm and wonderful. She didn't know what had happened in that flashing moment of anger, but it was a side of Joe that frightened her, a side that fed the one fear that had wedged itself like a burr into their relationship.

Joe ordered dinner for everyone, and Gilly stole glances toward the group as she moved about the carpeted room or rested back against the cool wall in the entryway. Joe was back in control, charming, orchestrating the conversation with wit and finesse.

Gilly leaned her elbows on the high reservation stand and traced the smile on his face with her eyes, willing it to stay there. *Your face wasn't meant for frowning, Joe. No . . . it was meant to be tossed back to the sun and wind, bold and rugged and daring. Not to be couched in lines that rob it of its grandness* . . . Joe Bennett was one of the most powerful men Gilly had ever met: powerful in physique, in work, even in his lovemaking, and it both awed and frightened her.

She thought back to his unexpected anger and knew instinctively what it was. Joe wanted to protect her. It was anger wrought out of caring and love. She shook her head without knowing it, her hair falling in soft folds about her shoulders. *No, Joe. Love me, but don't try to take away what I've worked so very hard for. Please, Joe* . . .

Gilly was in the kitchen saying good-night to the chef when Joe's party left. She walked across to the empty table, suddenly sad that she hadn't said good-bye.

"Good-night Gordon," she called across the room. "Now, go home to Ellie. She sees too little of you as it is!"

"Och, is it the romance expert talking here?" Gordon walked over and held out Gilly's coat for her. "And I say you see too little of life, my little one."

Gilly grinned. "Yes, you do say that. *A lot.*" She tipped her chin up. "But I'm just fine, Gordon. In fact—"

"In fact you are seeing Joseph Bennett. Good. That is what I wanted to hear."

Gilly lifted one brow.

"No, I do not snoop, Gilly. But either you are very fond of that gentleman, or you've been hired by the FBI to track his every move. The only time your eyes left him was when *he* was stalking *you!*"

Gilly laughed. "That obvious?"

Gordon nodded as he held the door for her. "Now, hurry quickly to your car and lock all the doors!"

Gilly threw him a kiss and breezed across the lot toward her ancient, dependable clunker.

The wind had picked up and leaves gusted across the concrete in the shadows of the neon lights. Gilly pulled up the collar of her coat and let the wind brush her hair back flat against the sides of her face. It felt good, like a refreshing shower, and she threw her head back to let the wind fully cleanse her and blow out all the day's cobwebs.

Breathing deeply, Gilly smiled to herself for no reason and began humming softly.

"Debussy. And I've never heard him hummed before. It's charming."

Gilly's head snapped around, the dangling notes carried off on the breeze. "Joe!"

He was leaning against the hood of his car, his arms folded loosely across his chest. "The harpist played that piece tonight. *Clair de lune,*" right?"

Gilly smiled and walked over to him. "Right. Do you think she could use an accompanist?"

"Gillian the Hummer. Sounds promising, if a bit lewd."

Before she could say another word, his lips covered her mouth with warm, hungry pressure.

"What are you doing standing out here?" she murmured as she finally pulled away.

"I came to pick you up."

"But I have my car."

Joe looked over her shoulder. "That's debatable."

Gilly wrinkled her nose. "She never breaks down."

"Good. Then she'll be movable in the morning when I have someone pick her up. I've already told your boss that I'm taking you home so he won't worry." He opened the door of his car.

She looked at Joe, his dark head bent, his hand holding the door for her to get in. The earlier anger was all gone, but the memory was still there, an unspoken veil between them.

"Just like that?" Gilly snapped her fingers.

Joe lifted his head and smiled. "Nope. I'll have to make a few phone calls."

"Where are your clients?"

"Back at the hotel. Gilly, I had to come back. I'm sorry for tonight. You surprised the hell out of me, that's all, and I don't react well to surprises." He paused, his eyes caressing her face. "I won't pretend to understand why you do the damnable things you do, but I do promise to try."

Gilly's face was still, bathed in the warmth of his look. She put her hand on his cheek and smiled softly. "Fair enough, Joe. And I'll try to diminish the surprises. . . ."

Gilly slipped slowly into the car and settled herself snug and tight against Joe's warm body. She rubbed her cheek along the wool of his jacket sleeve and breathed in the wonderful smell of him, her thoughts curling and tangling like smoky tendrils around her. *I'll try, Joe darling. And you'll try . . . and then?* Her brows drew together, her heart full, as she buried her unseen doubts in the shadowy comfort of his embrace.

CHAPTER NINE

"Hi, Joe, come on in!" Gilly yelled from the depths of the studio. "If you look hard, you'll find us buried here somewhere."

Joe strode casually into the dining room and looked around. Every surface was covered with white paper and overlays, and the floor sported more photographs than the Municipal Gallery.

"The wreck of the *Hesperus.*" He whistled through his teeth. "What's going on?"

"Instant fame and riches," Tugg joked. "A life of leisure, yachts, private islands in the sun—"

"Oh, shush, Tugg!" Gilly turned sparkling sapphire eyes on Joe. "We've been invited to *bid* on a job, Joe. A big one! It could put us in the big time."

"Mucho bucks," Tugg added, "in addition to the fame and glamor. We even get paid a respectable hunk for presenting, whether or not we get the job."

"That's great news. Congratulations."

"Well, that's a little premature, Joe. But who knows what tomorrow will bring?"

The enthusiasm lit up her lovely eyes, and Joe smiled into them. "Will you two still speak to me when you're rich and famous?"

"Oh, I don't know. What do you think, Tugg?" Gilly laughed giddily as she leafed through some sheets of press type.

"I think Joe's partially responsible for all this, so the answer is a definite yes."

Joe's head shot up. Tugg grinned and continued.

"He's fueled those creative juices in you so the sky's the limit! Besides the fact that it's nice to have someone around who understands how to stop work for meals and other such trivial but basic necessities."

Gilly glowered affectionately at Tugg, then looked over at Joe. "Well, don't you want to know who?"

"Who what?" Joe half sat on a tall stool, his long legs stretched out in front of him.

"Who invited us to work up a presentation."

"Oh, sure," he said quickly. "Who?"

"You two sound like a nest of owls!" Tugg complained from beneath a stack of prints.

Gilly laughed as she looked up from the sheets of type. *Who* is Gallagher and Sons. *The* Gallagher and Sons, fastest growing commercial real-estate firm in these parts, as Tugg would say. They do shopping centers, office buildings, and are now expanding into other states."

"So I hear. That's wonderful, Gilly. You and Tugg certainly deserve a shot at it."

"Well"—Gilly stepped over a color guide and came up alongside Joe, tucking her hand into the warmth of his arm—"I'm not sure Tugg and I would have picked such a huge outfit just yet, but since it kind of fell in our lap, it certainly can't hurt to try." She tilted her head and thick waves of reddish-streaked hair moved back from her flushed cheeks. "In spite of the way Tugg talks, we're not fooling ourselves. The competition is mighty stiff and we're awfully small potatoes."

Joe felt the familiar tightening in his limbs as she pressed against his hip. Every move she made stirred him these days, a look, a hand on his arm, even his own *thoughts,* damn it!

"Small potatoes, nothing!" Joe shifted on the stool to let Gilly slip into the small space between his legs and wrapped his arms around her waist. "You're top banana in my book." His breath tickled her neck. "When's the presentation?"

"A couple of weeks. It's going to be a crunch, but we'll make it." Joe's thumbs moved rhythmically against her waist and Gilly stilled them, unable to concentrate beneath the soft, sensuous pleasure.

"Are you open for suggestions?"

"Sure." She slipped out of his arms and dipped to the floor, straightening sketches.

"Why don't you take a break from your job at the Papillon? You're not going to be able to put your best work into this project if you spend nights over there."

Gilly's muscles tightened instinctively at his suggestion, a clear, unpleasant memory of his anger that night at the restaurant still fresh in her mind. Then reason took over, and she sat still for a minute, mulling over the thought. At last she looked up. "You may be right, Joe. I hate to do that to Gordon, but it's probably the best thing right now." She silently debated for another minute, then said, half aloud, "Yes, that's best. I'll call him first thing tomorrow."

Joe's satisfied smile went unnoticed.

"Hey, what's with all the racket?" Tugg straightened up from the corner of the room and and looked out the front window.

Joe stood up. "Almost forgot. That's just Timmy and Adam pulling things out of my car."

"Things? What kind of things?" Gilly looked at Joe suspiciously.

"Good things. When I called earlier, Timmy said he was starving and—"

"Timmy's *always* starving!"

"—so I stopped at the club and had them load the car with dinner."

A scraping noise in the hallway announced the Holmes-Bennett catering service. Covered carefully with fine white linens atop silver bowls, and set ceremoniously in the bottom of the Holmes wheelbarrow, was dinner. Timmy and Adam grinned proudly from behind the wooden handle of the old cart.

"Sure beats tuna, Mom!" Tim announced. "Even my brain thinks so!"

Gilly groaned, but was silenced immediately by the wafting threads of delicious-smelling food that filled the cluttered room: clams and hot croissants, chunks of juicy chicken in beautiful molded nests of potatoes, wine and salad and huge, gooey pieces of chocolate cake.

"Oh, Joe," Gilly murmured as Tugg lifted a white napkin and peeked beneath it at the tempting morsels, "you shouldn't have, but I'm so awfully glad you did! My stomach couldn't take one more doughnut or slice of cold pizza." She gave him a long, loving look.

He was doing it again, caring for her, making sure she ate, providing. . . . And yet she couldn't deny how good it felt—a wonderful, easing antidote to the hectic day. He hadn't done anything wrong, after all. She'd have done the same thing for starving friends, wouldn't she? *Of course she would!* her heart beat back loud and clear as she drifted to his side and hugged him close.

You're getting a little crazy, Gilly Holmes! And she was, in her thoughts, in the private times she spent thinking of Joe, loving him. It was almost as if it were too big a package to handle, this love that swelled her heart out beneath her rib cage until she was sure everyone could see it.

"You're quite a guy, Joe Bennett," she murmured into the cashmere wool of his sport coat.

"I was beginning to think you'd never notice."

If it hadn't been for Joe, Gilly knew she would never have gotten through the next two weeks. He fed them, carted an always-willing Timmy over to his house for meals with Adam and his mother, even helped Mary teach the cub scouts how to make cardboard turkeys! And somehow handled all of it, plus his own thriving business, with the ease of Superman.

For Gilly, life was so hectic, she didn't have much time to think. Which was a blessing, since it helped shove into the back of her busy mind any nagging uneasiness she had about the upcoming presentation.

But Tugg's curious questions flitting around the studio like pesty flies were another matter.

"Gallagher, et cetera, was written up again in this week's business journal, Gil."

"Terrific, Tugg. Maybe next week it'll be Holmes and Waters." She pulled gently on a loose piece of hair as she sat back and looked critically at the spec sheet.

"But why *us*, Gilly? How'd they ever think of us?"

Gilly's tired look peeped up from beneath a fringe of bangs. "Simple, my friend. Because we're terrific!"

"*I* know that, and *you* know that, but how in hell does Gallagher and Sons know that?"

Gilly shrugged. "Who knows? Maybe it was my host-essing smile. I've seen Gallagher often at Papillon, you know, and he probably said to himself, 'Hmmm, that young lady looks like she could work up an award-winning identity system. I'll have to find out who she is!' "

Tugg's rumbling laugh blew a paper onto the floor. "Possible, Gilly, but not probable."

Gilly nibbled on the end of a pencil, concentrating on the type composition before adding philosophically, "Well, who knows, Tugg? This isn't our first job, after all. We do have other clients."

Tugg watched her with a challenging grin on his face. "Sure, Gilly, that's it! Gallagher called that Chinese laundry whose sign we designed, or maybe that preschool over on Windsor, and asked them who in the world did their outstanding graphic design work!" Tugg popped a doughnut hole in his mouth.

"Well, the way I see it, it doesn't matter a whole hill of beans why they included us; what matters is how good our presentation is. So, perhaps if we put some of that Sherlock Holmes curiosity into these sheets of paper, we'll have half a chance to get the job!"

Tugg slapped her affectionately on the back as he advanced to the coffeepot. He took a long swig of hot coffee and turned his attention back to his best friend. "Hey, Gilly, don't get me wrong. I'm not going to turn my back on this job, just because I think it mighty strange we're in the running. No, sirree, I'm *not* one to look a gift horse in the mouth. I was just a little curious, that's all."

"Well, be curious about how we're going to get this done without adding seventeen more hours to each day, okay?" Gilly wrinkled her forehead and tried to throw him a menacing scowl.

"Sure." Tugg nodded, swallowing his smile. It was time to stop niggling and get back to the drawing board; Gilly was right. They ought to get the work done as soon as possible, because if his suspicions were correct, Gilly Holmes was going to be one angry lady very soon, and red-hot anger had a way of slowing down the creative process considerably.

CHAPTER TEN

"Are you sure you can't be there tomorrow, Tugg?"

"Don't see any way, Gilly, unless you want to throw away Petersen as a client. One of us *has* to go hold his icy-cold hand or we're going to lose the old bird's contract. And you know what they say about a bird in hand. . . ." He winked broadly. "Besides, you'd be much better off with Gallagher than I would. I hear he has an eye for beautiful honey-blondes." Tugg held a photo to the light.

Gilly looked down one last time at the comprehensives piled on the desktop. "Well, no matter what happens, we've given it our best shot."

"Right. We've done the best we can with what we have."

"Yes. I hear Studio Graphics is presenting, and they must have fifty people on their staff now. . . ."

"And we're just two . . ." Tugg stopped mid-sentence, his words hanging limply on the fading light of day.

Gilly looked at him. His returning stare lasted a brief minute before the two doubled over in laughter.

"We sound like two insecure know-nothings," Gilly said, gasping, the tears rolling down her cheeks.

"Two lost souls." Tugg's deep laugh filled the still room as he began to hum. "Our confidence ought to get us at least from here to the front door!"

"But I *am* confident." Gilly threw her narrow shoulders back and sucked in a gust of air defiantly.

"Right on! Me too!" And the two doubled over again, the week's tiredness pouring out through their silliness and laughter.

"Oh, my," Gilly said, brushing away the tears. "What's Joe going to think? I'm a mess! He'll be here in minutes to take me to dinner."

"Joe will think you're the most beautiful woman he's ever seen, just as he does every single time he steps into this room. And lately you've been looking mighty haggard at times! Love is blind, haven't you heard?"

Gilly sobered and looked over at Tugg. "Think so? How blind?"

"Hey, Gilly"—Tugg tossed his hands in the air— "don't go getting all serious on me. I have a nervous feeling you're aiming for *real* answers. I'm just a tired, worn-out photographer who doesn't know his head from a hole in the ground, much less have any expertise on affairs of the heart."

Gilly shook her head, smiling, and walked over to a wall mirror to inspect the damage of her laugh-tears. "Don't worry, Tugg, I won't make you play analyst. Besides," she added, running a brush over her thick hair, "it's not an analyst I need."

"Seems to me you don't need much, Gilly. He's a hell of a guy. And you've got me thrown in as a sidekick. Now, what more could any red-blooded woman want?"

Gilly grinned, then nodded, watching the face in the

mirror slowly nod back. *We all agree. Joe is a hell of a guy. And he's filling my life with a joy I never knew possible. . . . And I'm just a neurotic, thirty-year-old worrywart!* "Tugg, you know how much the business means to me?"

Tugg was silent for a minute. When he answered, his voice was kind and thoughtful. "Gilly, as I see it, the business *does* mean a lot to you, yes, but not in itself. It matters because it's living proof that Gilly Holmes is standing on her own two feet, handling her life, giving Timmy a good home. It means so much to you because it says you can do this all by yourself, and life isn't so scary anymore."

Gilly stared straight ahead, the mirror image blurring before her eyes. Slowly she turned toward Tugg. "Is that what you think?"

He shook his head, then looked frantically over his shoulder: "Anyone seen my soapbox?" When he looked back to Gilly the faint beginnings of a smile spurred him on. "Now that you've got me started, there just ain't no shuttin' me up! What else I think is this—that for some reason you are afraid Joe Bennett is going to take that independent feeling away from you. And without it life's going to seem scary again." He placed a hand on each of her shoulders and looked down into her face. "Personally, Gilly, I can't see it. But—"

"Tugg, enough." Gilly's voice was soft. When she raised her eyes, they were troubled, but shining again. "Tugg, you're a dear friend. But promise you'll never hang out a shingle for analysis—"

The sound of Joe's car at the curb broke into her words. She shrugged into her coat and started for the door, then turned back toward Tugg. "Because if you did, Mr. Waters, all your clients would fall in love with you, and then where would you be?"

"In heaven! Now, get going, and have fun, for tomorrow we may have an account that will keep us so busy we will never again enjoy life, love, or lust!"

"Stop! Tugg, go home and go to bed!" Gilly opened the door, her face flushed with new laughter.

"Night, Gilly!" He shoved her out the door and into the open, waiting arms of Joe Bennett, who had silently moved from his car to the bottom step.

"Ah, here she is, tumbling out the door into my arms —the woman who brings life to my life," Joe wrapped his arms around her with a dramatic flourish, then pulled her close and kissed her in a way that lit lone fires through her.

"Mmm, that feels sooo good." Gilly wrapped her arms around him, then looked back toward the door.

Tugg was still standing there, grinning broadly. "I'm right, aren't I?"

Gilly waved, then blew him a kiss. "Yeah, you're right, Dr. Waters. He's a hell of a guy." She grinned, pulled Joe close, and together they walked off to the car.

"I'm glad you picked Papillon's," Gilly said as they hurried through the brisk, black night and into the warmth of the restaurant. "It's been an eternity since I've seen Gordon."

"I'm sure he'll be anxious to see you." Joe turned to take her coat, letting his hands linger gently on her shoulders. Leaning over he whispered seductively into her hair, "Have I told you how beautiful you look tonight . . . ?"

Laughter bubbled up Gilly's throat as Tugg's words echoed in her ears.

Joe kept his head bent, kept his hands in place cupping her shoulders. "Not the correct response, Gillian. Try again."

"Give me a hint."

"Turn slowly, then throw your arms around me and

smother me in hot, sensuous kisses for being so terribly observant."

"Like this?" Gilly turned slowly, her eyes shining as they traveled slowly up his chest to his face. Tipping her feet forward she rose upward to meet the waiting crush of his lips.

Over his shoulder, Joe caught the amused smile of the hostess waiting at the door. "You're getting the idea. Perhaps we can get back to this later?"

Gilly grinned as she turned and innocently followed the hostess to the table.

The meal was wonderful, but even more wonderful was the man sitting across from her, loving her with his eyes. She reached for his hand and squeezed it gently.

"What's that for?"

"For being here for me. For helping me through these horrendous weeks, for understanding that there's a part of my life that I need to handle all by myself. . . ." She felt the tears build up and dabbed at them with the linen napkin. *That's it, Gilly, let all the emotions wrought of a sleepless week, a wonderful, loving man, a son you're crazy about, spill over onto Gordon's freshly laundered table- cloth in front of a roomful of strangers.* She swallowed hard. "What I mean is—"

Joe curled a finger beneath her chin and read into her deep blue eyes. "Shhh, I know what you mean, Gilly. And what *I* mean is that I love you very, very much." Before she could blink, he leaned over and kissed her gently, then settled back and committed to memory the lovely, shining look that fell from her eyes.

"Was that dessert?" she asked softly.

"Definitely not. Dessert will be even more memorable." He slipped his chair back and started to get up. "But before I get into that, I had better act like a businessman for a moment. There's a client across the room who has spotted me and I ought to say hello. Want to join me?"

Gilly shook her head. "I'd rather sit here and watch you from across the room—and dream about dessert. . . ."

Joe laughed at the seductive suggestion in her voice, and in long, loose strides wove his way across the room with Gilly's loving gaze heating his back.

"Gillian! How wonderful to see you!"

Gordon's deep, rich voice drew her attention back to the table.

"Gordon, hello! I was wondering where you were hiding yourself tonight."

"Och, behind stacks of paperwork, my dear. The torturous bain of my existence. Do you think Mr. Bennett could come up with a computer that could handle it all and leave me in peace?"

Gilly laughed. "I'm sure of it. Mr. Bennett can do anything, Gordon!"

"That's what your smile tells me, Gillian. I'm happy for you." He patted her hands with fatherly affection. "Now, tell me what's keeping you away from me."

"Well, it's exciting, Gordon. My partner and I have been invited to bid on a graphics design job with a *very* prestigious firm. It could be a wonderful thing for our tiny business."

"That's wonderful, Gillian. Congratulations! What is the firm?"

"Gallagher and Sons. You know Mr. Gallagher, Gordon, he's often in here for dinner—"

Gordon clapped his hands. "Of course I do! A good man." He winked at Gilly and added, "He must be a good man, right? Such a good friend of Mr. Bennett's, he is—"

Gilly's hand stopped in midair, her fingers wrapped

137

tightly round the icy water goblet. "Joe . . . Joe Bennett's friend?"

"Well, it makes good sense, Gillian. As I said to Ellie, two finer men you couldn't find in the business world. Honest as the day is long and—"

Gilly shook her head to clear the fog. Joe had never mentioned knowing Gallagher. "Friends?" Gilly set the water glass down.

"Your hearing giving you some problem, Gillian?" Gordon bent over with joking concern. "Sure they're friends, as best I can tell anyway. Don't tell me Gordon knows something about your gentleman friend that you don't know!" He winked and patted her arm.

Gilly smiled weakly. "Seems you do, Gordon. How . . . how do you know Joe and Mr. Gallagher are friends?"

Gordon threw back his balding head and laughed. "Oh, my, Gillian, owning a restaurant makes you privy to all *sorts* of information. Better than a hairdresser!" When Gilly didn't laugh along, he sobered and answered quickly. "They lunch here together occasionally. But that shouldn't put such concern on that pretty face, now, should it?"

Gilly shook her head. "No, Gordon." She took a drink of water, then wrapped both hands around the glass again and stared into it. Joe . . . and Gallagher know each other. Her body felt leaden, her heart heavy. Slowly she raised her head and looked up at Gordon. "Have . . . have they eaten here recently?" Gilly choked out the words, but she knew the answer before it ever reached her ears.

"As a matter of fact, yes. The last few weeks one, maybe two times, I can't be sure. So many customers, you know, Gillian . . ." His voice went on filling the hollow space between them while Gilly sat in her chair in stunned silence.

138

As Joe approached the table, he wondered why Gordon seemed to be having such a one-sided conversation with Gilly. The back of her head was as still as a painting, her fingers wound around her glass so tightly he was surprised it didn't snap in half. Perhaps she was slightly uncomfortable being a patron for a change, rather than hired help. But no, that wasn't the sort of thing that would bother Gilly one whit. Something else was wrong. He moved to his chair and looked at Gilly's face. *Terribly wrong.*

Gordon excused himself as a diner waved and beckoned him to his table.

Joe sat down and took a wild stab at nonchalance. "Well, Gilly, ready for the dessert before the dessert?"

Gilly lifted her eyes to his face and stared long and hard. Her lips were tense lines, her eyes beacons of accusation. "Joe," she said finally, her voice even and controlled, "are you responsible for the Gallagher presentation?"

Joe laughed lightly. "Hell, no, Gilly. You know I can't draw a straight line unless it's at the other end of a computer key."

"You know what I mean. Please answer me."

She released her hold on the glass and Joe was relieved. The image of those lovely fingers cut by broken glass was even more awful than the chill in her voice cutting its way to his heart. "All right, Gilly. No, I'm not responsible for the presentation. You and Tugg are. I am responsible for suggesting to Bernard Gallagher that he consider your firm along with the others. I considered it a favor to him, friend to friend. You two are good, creative graphic artists and would probably bid lower than larger firms. Bernie appreciated that, as I knew he would. Now, any more questions?"

Only her lips moved as she spoke. "No, no more questions." And Gilly pushed back her chair and walked out of the Papillon without another word. The only thought she allowed to enter her mind was that the night had turned an ugly black and was so very cold.

"For God's sake, you didn't even take your coat!" Joe yelled through the door as he tried to convince Gilly to let him in. "It's almost winter, you could get sick!"

"The cab was warm," she muttered through the crack. "And I was plenty hot, so I'm sure I'm fine. Now, go away, Joe."

"No. I refuse to step off this porch until you let me in, even if it means Mrs. Lewandowski finds me here in the morning and has to peel my frozen body from the ground. That would be a helluva thing for a nice, quiet mother of an eight-year-old to have to explain to the neighbors . . . and possibly the police!"

"Joe, I didn't know you had such drama in you." Her voice was tired and limp.

"There are plenty of things you don't know about me. Like, for instance, my patience runs mighty thin after midnight. So let me in or I'll break this damn door down! I swear it, Gilly—"

"Yes, you certainly do! All the neighbors are now at their windows wondering who Gilly Holmes's foul-mouthed visitor is. Come in, for heaven's sake!" She opened the door just wide enough for Joe to squeeze through.

"Why haven't you turned any lights on?" Joe asked as he stumbled into the tiny living room.

"I found the darkness more appropriate."

"Okay, suit yourself." He settled himself on the couch. "Don't you want to sit down?"

"Joe, why are you here?" Gilly walked over to the window and stared intently into the dark night.

"Because I love you, and there isn't a chance in hell I'd

let you walk away from me the way you did tonight without talking to you."

It wasn't his words that wrapped around Gilly's heart and tightened until she could barely breathe. It was the deep, husky pain that made everything else fade into the background. "Joe . . ." She turned slowly toward him.

Joe held out his arms. "Please, Gilly, talk to me?"

There wasn't a choice. It was that magnetic force that suspended free will, guiding Gilly down beside him where the warmth of his body held her as securely as chains. She slipped a space between them and looked up at him from eyes still swollen with tears. "Joe, why did you do it? Why? When you knew how important it was that you not interfere." She stared down at her hands lying limply in her lap. "Why, Joe?"

Joe held her gently. She seemed so vulnerable, like a very young child. He loved her so much, this woman who had brought sunlight back into his life. Loved her, and couldn't bear the thought of hurting her.

"Gilly, I'll try to explain, but you have to promise me you'll open your mind a little, and listen to what I'm saying." Joe rubbed his fingers up and down her arm as he spoke, a soft, soothing motion.

Gilly nodded slowly, too tired to call back the anger that had eaten away inside her.

"A few weeks ago an old friend of mine called. He was opening up a real estate company out in Bucks County."

"Joe, that's very nice, but I don't see—"

"Shhh, trust me." Joe covered her lips with his finger, then let his hand slip to her neck as he laced his fingers through her hair. "He asked me to remember him if I knew of anyone looking for a house. I sent two new employees out to see him and he's found both of them the house of their dreams. Everybody's happy."

"Joe, I know what you're saying, but it's not quite the same." She looked into his eyes. "Don't you see? The

141

only reason Gallagher asked us was because you asked him to! You used your friendship to get us favored treatment, and I don't run my life that way, Joe, *or* my business!" She could taste the anger coming back, but this time it churned in an excruciating way, mixed painfully with the overwhelming love she held in her heart for Joe Bennett.

"Gilly, my darling Gilly . . ." Joe brushed a kiss into her hair. "You're not giving anyone the least damn bit of credit for anything. Bernie Gallagher wouldn't do business with a less-than-outstanding firm if his mother begged him on bended knees. He's a nice guy, but a hard-nosed businessman. Sure I suggested he look into Holmes and Waters, but there's no way in hell he'd have sent the notice if he didn't think you had a leg to stand on." One hand continued to play lovingly with her hair, while the other slipped over and covered her hands still lying in her lap. "And you haven't given me any credit, either—I'd never shove off poor talent on a friend." His hand slipped beneath hers, down to her thigh, and with gentle, firm fingers he rubbed the silky dress material back and forth. "Not even one I was crazy in love with . . ."

Gilly's head felt fuzzy, her body light, no longer burdened by the heavy press of anger. "Joe, you don't fight fair." She gasped as he slid his hand beneath the hem of her skirt and kneaded the warm, moist skin beneath.

"Sorry, love," he murmured as his fingers moved ever so slowly on the tender skin between her legs. "Let's finish that business, then. Besides all the logical, sensible, argument-proof reasons I've given you, there's one other."

Gilly tilted her head toward his, one hand moving slowly across his chest. "What is it?" she whispered.

"I love you. I love you very much, Gilly Holmes," Joe's voice was a soft, delicious caress against her cheek. "And I care for you so much that this force inside of me takes over sometimes, makes me do things that makes the woman of my dreams angry—"

"Furious," she whispered raggedly in between heated kisses. "Promise, Joe . . ."

"On my honor, my best cub-scout honor, Gilly . . ."

His fingers still moved beneath her dress, lightly stroking the soft, sensual regions, and Gilly felt the threads of reason quickly evaporating. ". . . promise me that you will try never, *ever* . . . ohh, Joe." She gasped, the room swaying.

"I do, dear, Gilly, I do. . . ." Joe curled her closer against his heated body, the hammering of her heart pressing against his chest. "Oh, my lovely Gilly," he whispered on ragged breath as his fingers inched slowly upward beneath her clothing until only a thin, lacy layer of fabric separated them from the throbbing center of her desire.

"Joe." Her voice was a haunting melody now, full of passion and love.

"Yes, my love . . ." He slowly rotated his thumb, his fingers gently cupping her.

"Do you know how much I love you?" Her fingers wound into his hair as she lay back against the cushions of the couch, pulling Joe close until he blanketed her body.

"How much?" Joe smiled through his haze, looking rapturously into eyes as bright as the sky on a clear summer night.

" 'Let me count the ways,' " she breathed, her voice lilting, drifting off. . . .

Joe's husky laugh cushioned her as he cradled her beneath him, his hands tilting her sideways as he slipped the silk blouse from her arms and slid her skirt into a soft, shimmering puddle at the foot of the couch. "While you count, my love, I will show you. . . ."

Moonlight guided him as he laid his clothes in a heap

on the polished floor, then molded his body next to Gilly's on the deep, worn couch. Moonlight shadowed her nakedness, and Joe's eyes traced each hollow of darkness, each stripe of pale, beautiful flesh. He cupped one lush breast in his hand, then circled the other slowly, dropping kisses along the hot trail left by his fingers. The eager prickling of her nipples brought a delighted smile to his lips.

"Oh, Joe." Gilly's waiting arms encircled him, scooping up handfuls of thick black hair as she held him close. Her hands moved slowly down him, anxious to explore every curve of his body. "Why is it you make me so very angry one minute, and then can carry me off on a cloud the next?"

"It must be the way of love."

"Is that the way we're going?" She kissed the bareness of his chest, her tongue moving in tiny circles, loving the taste and feel of him. His brown nipples stiffened in her mouth.

Joe's voice was ragged with desire. "An understatement, my love. Decidedly an understatement. We're already there." He rolled over, gently pulling her beneath him and slowly spreading her legs with one hand. His fingers lingered there for a moment until Gilly moaned, her body arching toward him.

"Joe, I love you! Oh, my darling, Joe—" and with arms wrapped around his back and a torrent of passionate kisses sprinkled in the hollow of his neck, she urged him to enter her.

He came into her slowly, his body coiled as tightly as a spring. A light sheen of sweat dotted his forehead and his black eyes were deep and dusky with need. "I never thought"—Joe's voice was so husky Gilly could barely make out his words—"I never thought this was waiting for me. I never dreamed—"

Gilly arched against his body, her mind whirling in

some faraway, star-studded sky. "Neither did I, my darling, neither did I."

As he buried himself deep within her, they soared together, carrying each other beyond their wildest dreams.

CHAPTER ELEVEN

Gilly stepped into the spacious atrium and looked around.

This was worse than her first date! She patted her cheek absently with one shiny palm and grimaced. Wet! Her hands were wet! She leaned her thick portfolio against a huge potted plant, then gently placed the daisy Timmy had given her for good luck down next to it and pulled a Kleenex out of her purse. She wiped her hands furiously. Then she looked down at her tailored emerald-green suit and smoothed out an imaginary wrinkle. *Now, Gilly,* she scolded, *it's time to calm down.* She brushed a lock of hair back into place and grinned at no one in particular.

Checking her watch Gilly took a deep breath. Time to meet the friendly dragon. With a show of confidence she collected her belongings, wished herself well, and headed for the elevator at the end of the marble lobby.

"Good mornin'."

Gilly jumped. Joe? And he had promised, he had *sworn*, he wouldn't come. Gilly looked up into the smiling eyes of the elevator man. She blushed furiously, then smiled back. He didn't look or sound anything like Joe. This was a major case of paranoia! Why couldn't she shake the feeling that Joe might, at any minute, dart out from behind a plant, or appear out of thin air right in the middle of her presentation?

But those were silly fears, weren't they? Her thoughts slipped back over the hours and their wondrous evening together. After making love they had wrapped themselves in blankets and sat pressed together before the fire sharing dreams and fears as they sipped hot cocoa. Joe had listened so very hard, and Gilly had, too, trying desperately to understand his intense need to wrap her in protective folds. But just as she'd be tottering on the brink of understanding, it would fall away, leaving her with a nagging feeling that something was going unsaid, something so big and powerful that it controlled the actions of this wonderful man whom she loved with her whole heart and soul.

The elevator man watched her curiously, this lovely blonde who seemed to be eyeing his lift as if it were made of plastic. "Been workin' this one since seventy-eight and it's never as much as lurched," he said proudly, hoping to wipe the worry off her pretty face.

Gilly's head snapped up and she stared at him for an instant; then her face broke into a wide smile. She laughed softly. "That's wonderful, thank you for telling me." And she walked confidently into the waiting box. "Gallagher and Sons, please."

Gilly looked at her watch as she walked off the elevator two hours later. *Why does it seem like I've been up there for six hours?* She took a deep, refreshing breath and felt the muscles in her back begin to relax, the tight,

147

crinkly feeling in her face subside. *Ahhh, that feels so much better!*

The lobby was much busier now than it had been midafternoon when she had arrived. People filed in and out the wide front door and stood around in small groups talking while dozens of well-dressed men and women walked purposefully across the wide lobby, briefcases and attachés clutched tightly in hand. Gilly smiled as she watched them, enjoying the panoply of color that streamed before her eyes.

Slowly the weeks' tense buildup eased its way out of her bones and the warm flush of blood ran freely through her body once again. *There. I'm all intact again!* The last traces of tension from her face were washed away by a lovely warm smile. Several gentlemen turned their heads and grinned back. *Good Lord*— she chuckled to herself— *I better watch out or I'll be arrested for soliciting!*

Her gaze switched to a young man in blue jeans who had slipped in the wide front doors when the guards weren't looking and now peddled his wares freely from behind the protection of a huge ficus tree. Gilly laughed at the audacity of youth, then pulled a bill out of her purse and looked over his collection.

"You have quite a variety! What would you suggest for my eight-year-old son?"

The fellow grinned amicably. "How about one of these?" He waved a monkey-on-a-stick in the air. "Give him an idea what things were like in the olden days."

Gilly laughed. The "olden days" for the salesman were when she was in college! "Terrific. I'll take it."

And then she spotted a fluffy black-and-white windup dog. When the key was turned, the dog strutted, barked, then somersaulted crazily. Gilly laughed aloud. Adam! She could just see the glinting light in his eyes and hear the husky giggles as he paraded the silly dog across the kitchen floor in front of the cook.

148

"And I must have one of these too!" She paid for the items quickly, then stuck the bag down next to her portfolio and looked back into the lobby.

Now what? Tugg! She'd almost forgotten, she should call Tugg and give him the news.

She scanned the spacious lobby looking for a pay phone.

Gilly's heart flipped over three times. She pinched her eyes shut and pressed her palm flat against her chest to calm the wild fluttering, then looked up again. He was still there, it wasn't a mirage at all.

Joe stood across the room beneath a huge clock, his black eyes glued to the elevator. Gilly watched invisibly from behind the tree, her eyes swallowing this wonderful hulk of man who was supposed to be at his office closing million-dollar deals. But no, he was here, waiting in the lobby like an expectant father, waiting for Gilly to step off the elevator so he could sweep her up in his arms. She picked up her portfolio and walked quickly over to him.

His face was a study in concern. Gilly smiled softly. *Study in Concern* . . . yes, she could sketch those fine lines with her eyes closed, the thoughtful lines that creased his brow, the firm set to his chin, the tiny indentation in his left cheek, the prominent bones that shaped the lovely whole. Would she never tire of painting him across her mind and heart?

"Gilly!" His arms reached out to her as she neared, his face relaxing in a rush of love. He circled her with his arms, packages and all, and hugged her close. "Well," he said, releasing her at last, "did old Bernie treat you right?"

She dropped her packages to the floor and slipped the lapels of his topcoat between her fingers, smiling up into his eyes. "He treated me just fine, Joe."

"You got the job!"

"No."

149

"No?"

"No." She smiled softly.

Joe stood back to scan her face. She wasn't fooling. "You *didn't* get the job?" His deep voice rumbled across the lobby and several passersby stopped to stare. With difficulty Joe lowered his voice. "What do you mean, you didn't get the job?"

Gilly tried to smile away his concern. "I mean that Holmes and Waters is too small a firm to meet the time constraints of this job, Joe. It rightfully went to a much larger firm."

"The hell it did!" Joe released his hold on Gilly's arm and headed for the elevators, incoherent mumblings trailing behind him.

Gilly dropped her portfolio and rushed after him, grabbing him by the arm. "Where are you going?"

"To talk to Bernie Gallagher myself!"

"Why?" Gilly's eyes flashed.

"Because he doesn't know that you can hire the extras to see that the job gets done, that's why." Joe started to pull away.

"But I can't do that, Joe. I don't even *want* to do that!"

Joe turned at the intensity in her voice, and Gilly took the opportunity to pull him back out of traffic.

"Joe . . ." she said softly but with warning.

"I know," he said, the anger slowly evaporating. "I'm doing it again, aren't I?"

A smile broke the lines of Gilly's lips. He sounded like a boy, a gallant little schoolboy whose efforts at winning the playground war have just been crushed. She touched a palm to his cheek, her eyes glistening. "Joe, it's okay. It's all for the best. Really, because—"

"But you *are* good. They're passing up a good thing, Gilly."

"No, they're not." Her eyes twinkled mischievously.

"They're not?" Joe wrapped his arms around her.

"Nope. They hired us to do an identity profile for a shopping mall in Denver. It's a much smaller job in scope, but will give Tugg and me a lot of exposure. It's great. Tugg will be thrilled, and I am too. That other would have kept me at the drawing board forty-seven hours a day. Had you considered that, Joe?"

He bent his head low until there was barely enough space between them to speak. "No, I hadn't. I would have slain that dragon when it reared its ugly head."

The words tickled her cheek, and when the laughter bubbled up her throat, Joe's lips were there to catch it.

"You're shameless."

"Never was before. But I seem to be leaning that way. Must be the company I keep." He picked up her things, spun her around, and tucked her into the circle of his arm. "Come on."

"Where are we going?"

"Where are we going?" He threw back his handsome head and laughed. "The charming lady wants to know where we're going? To celebrate, my love, to celebrate!" And this time he did pick her up, clear off the ground, as one strong arm circled her waist and twirled her in a half circle that delighted the crowd of a dozen or so that had stood aside to watch.

As they drove out of the parking lot, Joe picked up his portable phone and handed it to Gilly. "Here."

Gilly took it and smiled into it. "Hello, phone. I wouldn't accept cooks, so now he gives me phones. Nice . . ."

"Funny lady, call Tugg."

Gilly grew serious. "Of course! Thank you, Joe, I nearly forgot. He'll be waiting on pins and needles to hear what happened."

"After you tell him the news, have him bring Timmy, and both of them can meet us at my house around six. I'll let Mom and Adam know and we'll all party together."

"Aye, aye, sir!"

"Now, before you start gabbing, tell me where to go for perfect steaks, sourdough bread, and sacher torte."

"Um, let's see. Who's treating?"

"Me."

"Okay." Gilly grinned. "Try August's Prime Beef on Southwark and Hugo's in Germantown."

Joe cocked one brow. "And if *you* were treating?"

She grinned and quickly dialed Tugg's number, mumbling over the mouthpiece. "Bert's Market and doughnuts at the second-day bread store."

Joe grimaced. "I'll have to remember that."

Gilly tilted her head and covered the mouthpiece with her hand. "You know, for a onetime street kid, you have mighty fine tastes."

"I come by it naturally. My mother would feed us beans for weeks to have one meal of the best prime steaks in Pittsburgh. Now I just skip the beans."

He laughed and headed the car toward August's, filled with an incredible euphoria that he silently prayed would never go away.

CHAPTER TWELVE

"Why didn't they just get a flag from Montgomery Ward? I think that's where we got ours." Jimmy Webster pulled off his neckerchief and stuffed it into the pocket of his jeans.

"Because, nutso, Ward's wasn't here!"

"Sure, Jerry. It's right next to McDonald's."

"Yeah, but not during the Revolutionary War!" Stanley loved history and knew all about the Revolutionary War.

"Well, I bet my Gram could make a flag like Betsy Ross did," Adam said quietly.

The other scouts nodded agreeably from their seats in the Holmes station wagon. If anyone could make a flag like Betsy Ross, Gram Bennett could.

Gilly smiled from her invisible post as driver. That was one of the things she liked best about field trips: the boys forgot she was there and talked freely. She was sorry Mary Bennett hadn't come along; the praise would have tickled her.

"How much longer till we get home, Mom? I could eat a whole cow!" Timmy yelled during a rare acknowledgment of Gilly's presence.

"Soon, Timmy. Just a few more minutes on the highway." *If the traffic doesn't get any worse,* she thought to herself. She regretted having planned the Betsy Ross House trip for after school. The return trip put them right in the middle of rush-hour traffic! But Saturdays wouldn't be much better, she supposed. Oh, well. She'd know better next time.

A low rumble from the engine drew her forward on the seat. She gripped the wheel tightly and listened. There it was again, a slow grinding noise coming from somewhere beneath the hood. She slowed the car and pulled off onto the shoulder.

"Hey, where are we?" Stanley yelled, looking out the back window.

"Somebody has to, you know, *go,*" Adam suggested wisely.

"Mom?" Tim leaned over the front seat.

Gilly smiled. "Nothing to worry about. Clunker groaned a little, and I just want to check her out. Stay calm, men!" she teased as she turned the ignition off. "Be back in a second."

Gilly pulled her coat tightly around her to keep out the chill wind. She stood somberly in front of the car, staring into its belly. Everything looked okay, she decided, not that she was too sure what that meant. But nothing was steaming. She had just had a new battery put in, and the oil changed. *It's probably just a loose screw,* she decided, and quickly got back into the warmth of the car. "Okay, home it is!" she yelled back to the scouts, and flipped the key in the ignition.

Nothing happened.

Gilly stared down at the traitorous switch and turned the key again. The engine was dreadfully silent.

154

Nibbling on her bottom lip Gilly turned around. Nine pairs of huge, wondering eyes fell into hers.

"Well, fellas, Clunker seems to be taking a nap."

Timmy shook his head. "It's okay, Mom. Don't worry. We can push!"

"Yeah!" the scouts chorused, and started to scramble for exits.

"No, wait!" Gilly's voice settled them back. "No. Just stay put. There'll be a policeman by in a minute or two and he'll take care of everything."

"Will he have a gun?"

"Will we get to ride in the paddy wagon?"

"Will you get in trouble?"

The last was a worried whisper from Adam that brought a soft smile to Gilly's lips. She folded her elbows across the back of the seat and assured the boys everything would be fine, just a bit of an adventure, that's all.

When the boys were settled, she got out of the car and lifted the hood so a squad car would notice her. *Oh, Joe,* she thought suddenly, *I wish you were here!* The thought brought a smile to her freezing lips. She'd expended such effort keeping Joe from taking over, and who was the first person she thought about when she needed help? *Maybe it's because just the thought of him warms me clear through,* she decided as she shoved her cold hands deep into her pockets.

Ten minutes later she was still thinking of Joe, the scouts were getting cold and restless, and there hadn't been a police car in sight.

Time to reassess the situation, she decided with a grimace. Looking around to determine exactly where they were, Gilly took note of the tall, protective fence that bordered the highway. There was no way off until the next exit, which was, she calculated quickly, about a quarter of a mile down the road. That wouldn't be too bad. The boys could walk that easily enough, and the

Standard station was just off the exit. Yes, that would be much better than sitting there until heaven knows when and having everyone worried sick about them.

"Fellows," she called over the seat, "we're going to do something a little adventurous today."

The boys took to the challenge like fish to water, and Gilly decided in short order that they all deserved a medal of honor. From her position at the rear of the single line, she led the arrow-straight formation in marching songs and the group trooped briskly and merrily along the shoulder of the highway toward the exit.

"There she is, men!" she called at last, pointing toward the exit sign. "We're almost there!"

A screech of tires collided with her words, and Gilly jumped, her heart leaping to her throat. "Boys, move to the right!"

The driver of a small sports car had passed them by, then screeched to a stop, spinning gravel in all directions, and was now backing up on the highway.

Maybe someone was finally going to offer to help them, Gilly thought optimistically. Too bad they'd almost been run over in the process! She rubbed her hands together for warmth and watched as the car pulled to a stop and a striking-looking woman stepped out, then walked quickly toward the group that was now huddled on the muddy slope next to the shoulder.

"What are you doing here?" The woman stared at the clump of scouts, her voice a mixture of surprise and irritation.

Gilly started to speak, then stopped as one small boy stepped forward, his eyes large and meeting the woman's gaze reluctantly.

"Hello, Mother." Adam's voice was barely a whisper.

Gilly's mouth dropped open, then snapped closed as she watched the well-dressed woman walk over and put an arm around Adam's shoulders. She kissed him on the cheek then held him by each small shoulder. "Adam, answer me. What are you doing in this terrible weather, walking along a highway?"

Finally Adam was able to collect himself enough to seek out Gilly. "Ummm, Gilly . . . ?"

The woman stood up and faced her accusingly. Gilly was swept with a strange jumble of emotions at meeting Joe's former wife for the first time. She pinched her cold fingers together. But this certainly wasn't the time to deal with *that!* Stepping forward she held out her hand. "Hello. I'm Gilly Holmes, Adam's den mother."

The woman raised one fine brow.

"Let me explain this."

"Please," she said in a cold, demanding tone.

Gilly stumbled on, angry with herself for feeling nervous. "We had a little car trouble coming back from a field trip and couldn't seem to get anyone to help us. We're on our way to the gas station."

Gilly wanted to stop talking, wanted the woman to say something, *anything,* but Adam's elegant mother stood in silence.

"Yeah, Mother," Adam mustered. "We're on our way home. Where're *you* going?"

The woman wrapped her fur coat more closely around herself. "I just got back in town, Adam. And I was coming to see you." She smiled at Adam and her face softened. "But I didn't expect to find you *here.* Is this what cub scouts do? Does your father know about this?"

"I do apologize," Gilly broke in, "and I hate to interrupt, but the boys are freezing and I'm very anxious to get them off the highway."

"Of course." She was cool, but polite. "I will take Adam with me."

Gilly looked down at Adam, who was now pressed against her side. She put one hand on his shivering shoulder and looked back up at his mother.

157

"I don't think that's wise. His . . . his father thinks he's with me, so perhaps you could see him when he gets back to his house ar—"

"No. I'm taking Adam with me." Her back had stiffened and her beautifully made-up eyes flashed with sudden anger. "Adam is my son. He will come with me." The cool, even tones were knife sharp, and Gilly found herself shivering.

"I understand your feelings, but it would be better for everyone—"

"Better? Trooping this child along a murderous highway in this miserable weather is better than my driving him safely home?" Her jaw was set in a pouting challenge.

Adam looked up into Gilly's face. "Gilly," he said softly, "it's okay. I'll be fine." He walked over to his mother and stood still at her side. "See you, guys." His face was expressionless except for his eyes.

Turned toward Gilly they begged her not to say anything, begged her not to embarrass him in front of the kids. *He's afraid of his mother making a scene,* she thought. *The poor little kid doesn't want to be in the middle of a fuss.*

Gilly shook her head, a cold chill filling her clear through her body. She'd die before she'd hurt Adam. Why, oh, why did children have to suffer for grown-ups' errors?

Without interfering further she watched the elegant woman and the small boy walk quickly back to the sports car and watched the spray of gravel fly through the cold air as the car sped off down the highway.

Gilly was left with a cold, grasping feeling that attached itself to her, then pulled as tightly as an iron chain around her heart.

But looking back, nothing she had felt on the highway, not the chill, the fear, or the cold wind filling every hollow of her body, could have prepared Gilly for what she experienced that evening.

"Timmy, sit closer to that fire." She put another log on the flames and brought Timmy a glass of hot chocolate.

"Hey, thanks, Mom! This is terrific service. Let's get stuck on the highway more often!"

"No, thank you." Gilly wrapped her worn robe tightly around herself, then settled down next to him. "That was definitely not my idea of an ideal field trip."

"Whatcha worried about? We're all safe."

"Worried?"

"Yep. You've got those funny little lines around your mouth and there's a thing right here"—he touched her neck with one finger—"that kinda throbs when you're worried."

Gilly hugged him. "Don't be silly."

Timmy threw her a you-can't-fool-me look and turned his attention back to the *Cosby Show*.

Gilly pulled her legs up beneath her and stared unseeing at the screen. Why didn't Joe call? She'd called Mary immediately and explained what had happened. Mary said not to worry, everything would be fine. But Gilly had an unsettling feeling that things were far from fine.

Gilly shivered and wrapped her arms around herself.

It was Henry who nudged Gilly out of a half-sleep hours later, worrying her arm gently.

"What is it, boy, what's wrong?" She looked around the room. Timmy had gone to bed hours before, and it was just she and the dog and the dying fire.

Seconds later the shrill ring of the doorbell echoed through the sleepy house, and Gilly's heart lurched. Before she could get to the door, it rang again, the dissonant, insistent sound frightful against the backdrop of night.

With Henry pressed against her side, Gilly stood

159

shivering in the hallway. "Who is it?" she called tentatively through the locked door.

"Joe."

Joe! She threw the door open wide, the gust of cold air nearly knocking her over. "Joe! Oh, Joe, I've been so worried." She pulled him into the hallway and closed the door behind him.

He stood still, his body stiff and unresponsive to her hug. Gilly felt a tightness around her heart. Adam! The blood drained slowly from her face and her knees grew weak beneath her. She held on to the door frame for support, her large eyes searching Joe's face. "Adam . . . oh, Joe, is Adam all right?"

"Adam is fine, Gilly." The words were clipped, short, and came from a face masked in chilly anger. "He's just fine, but he could have been killed, Gilly!"

"Joe, what are you talking about?" Gilly stepped back against the wall, her head spinning. What was going on here? "His mother—?" She didn't even know what questions to ask.

"His mother brought him home. That in itself was upsetting. But wasn't even a runner-up for the rest of the news, that you had let my son walk along a highway . . . in traffic that . . ." He shook his head, his dark hair falling over his forehead. There was anguish in his voice when he spoke again. "He could have been killed, Gilly. My only son could have been killed! And you too"—his voice choked out the words—"and Timmy. What in God's name were you doing? What were you thinking of? What kind of a mother are you?"

Gilly's eyes widened as his words registered. Her stomach churned from the strength of the verbal blow and she swallowed painfully around the horrible flow of tears that threatened to choke her. "Joe Bennett, how can you say such a thing to me! What kind of mother am I? The best kind I can be! And I try damn hard." Her hands flew to her hips, her back arching as strength slowly ebbed back into her whipped body. "Who are *you* to attack my parenting?"

Joe bristled, but Gilly didn't give him time to speak.

"You shelter Adam until sometimes I think you're going to choke him. I don't know why you do it, Joe. . . ." Her voice began to break, but Gilly wasn't through. She forced in a huge lungful of air and continued while the thoughts were still clear. "It's as if there are two parts to you, the kind, loving, witty Joe that I love, and the other, this Joe"—she jabbed unthinkingly at his chest—"this person I can't begin to understand, who wants to wrap everyone he loves in protective wrap, just like Mary's chickens! Who wants to—"

"That's enough, Gilly!"

Gilly fell silent and looked sadly into his eyes, the tears slowly falling down her cheeks. Breath and strength slowly left her. She felt shriveled and dried up.

"Oh, Joe, it's far more than enough. . . ." With all the strength she could muster, Gilly turned and walked slowly toward her bedroom, leaving Joe standing alone in the deathly chill of the dark hallway.

Curled in a lifeless bundle beneath the heavy quilt, Gilly gave herself up to sleep, numb and unable to think after the defeating events of the day. The dark hours swept her up, healing, soothing, calming while she slept.

"Gilly . . ." A soft tapping on the door filtered into the quiet room hours later.

Gilly rolled over on her side, pulling the blankets up to her ears. Morning sounds were intruding, but she didn't want to give in to them. Not yet. She fell back into a half slumber.

Joe . . . he'd filled her night, even in sleep. As she opened her eyes, she saw him, too, standing in the bright light of morning. Her heart swelled. She loved him so very much.

161

The gentle tap, like a tiny bird on a windowpane, came again against her bedroom door. "Gilly . . . ?"

It was a ragged whisper, familiar and strange at once. She sat up, startled, pulling the covers up to her chin and staring at the door.

"Gilly? May I come in?"

Gilly's heart lurched, then she nodded slowly. "Yes. Yes, Joe."

He stood in the door frame, a heavy stubble shadowing his face, his long body rumpled in day-old clothes, bare feet stretched along the cold floor.

"Oh, Joe." Gilly reached out for him. "Were you . . . were you here all night?"

He nodded with a half smile. "Henry and I shared the couch. He got the lion's share."

"All night?"

"Yeah. I started out alone, but—"

"No, silly. Were you here all night?"

Her smile slowly soaked through the cold that had filled him the past long hours. He nodded, shoving his hands deep into the limp pockets of his suit pants. "Didn't sleep much. I wanted to be here when you woke up." His voice was drained of energy, the voice of someone who had watched the moon until it finally gave way to dawn. His thoughts had stretched as long as the night, one long, continuous thought of Gilly Holmes, and how he couldn't stand it if she walked out of his life, couldn't bear the pain of losing another loved one. "Will you talk to me?"

Gilly nodded slowly and motioned for him to come to her. "Of course I will, Joe."

He sank down on the mattress and swallowed her hands between his own.

Gilly watched him, her eyes brimming with love. They'd work this out, somehow. They *had* to work it out.

She loved this puzzling man. "If you hadn't been here, I would have tracked you down until I found you, Joe."

"And what would you have said?" He leaned back against the pillows, cradling her in the curve of his arm.

"I'd probably have begun by telling you how much I loved you, you crazy fool."

"Excellent beginning." His husky voice was choked with emotion.

"Then I'd have followed up by telling you I know you spoke and acted out of love . . . love for all *three* of us."

Joe nodded, the pressure of his tousled head firm against her cheek. "Yes, but I guess sometimes I'm a bit harsh and relentless in that love. Henry and I came to that decision around daybreak."

"Yes, you and Henry were right." A smile lifted her voice. "And if you weren't such an incredibly sexy, wonderful person under all that, I'd probably be wondering how I let myself fall in love with you."

Joe cupped her chin and turned her head until she looked at him fully. "But, Gilly, it was wrong. The danger, the—"

"I know you think that, Joe, but sometimes life presents dangers and you deal with them the best way you can. I didn't *plan* for Clunker to give up the ghost, Lord knows! You can't hide from dangers, Joe. Sometimes you have to do things, even knowing they might occur."

"But you can anticipate."

"And then cancel? Cancel that part of living?"

"Sometimes, yes."

Gilly ran her fingers through his hair. *No . . . no, you didn't cancel living. She didn't—*

"Gilly." Joe captured her hand and drew it to his lips. "Gilly, we'll work this out. The course of love . . ."

Gilly smiled and lay back against his chest. "Yes, my darling, but ours isn't just another 'not smooth' course.

Sometimes I think we're trailblazing through the Rockies."

Joe smiled and nuzzled her hair. "Uh-huh. In January."

"Yes, that's it." She pressed her head into the hollow of his neck, her throaty laughter wrapping around him.

Joe shifted his weight until he cradled her full against him, his arms wound around and resting beneath her breasts. "So, we'll just build a magnificent fire, and warm ourselves, and we'll get through those mountains, my love, we will. And sail off on the other side of smooth, wonderful waters."

"What about sea storms, Joe?" she whispered.

"We'll build a strong boat, my love."

CHAPTER THIRTEEN

"Mary, this is terrific. What spoiled little scouts we're going to have!"

"That's what grandmothers are for, dear." She patted Gilly's shoulder and watched the activity in the front of the Bennetts' little theater. "Isn't it fun?"

Gilly smiled back. Yes, it was. The Bennett household was a bit turned on its head, but it was fun.

A huge puppet stage filled the front of the room, and nine happy scouts ran about like elves, practicing lines, jabbing one another with colorful hand puppets that Mary had painstakingly sewn together, and giggling when the turkey puppets nibbled on the pilgrims' noses.

The show had been the boys' and Gilly's idea, but the elaborate finishing touches were definitely due to Gram's incredible imagination. Tomorrow they'd load up the whole kit and caboodle and present their very own Thanksgiving show to the young patients at Children's Hospital.

"Joseph should be here to see this. It would make him beam to see Adam on top of the world this way."

"Yes, yes, it would." Yes, Joe should be here. He had been gone three days out of a four-day business trip, and Gilly had never anticipated the depth of loneliness that now enveloped her. Perhaps it was because of the incredibly wonderful weeks they'd had since that awful day of the highway march. They'd both thrown themselves fiercely into loving one another, forcing away the fears and disagreements. The days had been filled with phone calls and flowers, the nights with stolen moments of love. Joe's sudden appearances in the studio were as frequent as Tugg's jokes, and his deep, rich laughter brought warmth from the chilling winds of the Philadelphia November.

Gilly had never known such happiness. It was a wonderful gift that she savored and cherished moment by moment by moment.

"Gilly, your glow has made this house a home." Mary patted her arm as if somehow privy to the thoughts running through the young woman's head. "Finally."

"Oh, Mary." Gilly laughed, a blush painting her cheekbones a lovely rosy hue. "Your being here has a little to do with it, you know! After all, I don't live here."

"No." She turned and looked at Gilly seriously through clear, dark eyes that were a mirror of her son's. "But you should, Gilly. You and Timmy belong here."

Gilly was taken aback. Mary had been a silent observer to their courtship, never forcing her opinions on either of them. She had wrapped Gilly in her love, but had always remained silent when it involved Joe. "Mary," Gilly said softly, "I don't know what to say."

"Then that's the best time to be silent." She nodded with smiling eyes. "I don't mean to interfere, and I *won't* interfere, but it's the truth."

Gilly smiled. "Do you really think Joe would be able

to put up with an opinionated female who's stubborn and willful and—"

Mary's laughter circled the room. "Of course! Look at his mother!"

Gilly hugged her close in happy understanding as they watched three of the cub scouts tumble over the front of the puppet stage, sending Indians and corn scurrying across the stage.

Finally the boys settled down and Mary and Gilly played audience to a most successful dress rehearsal. Turkeys and pilgrims and Indians cavorted delightfully across the colorful stage and joined together en masse to sing the boys' finale choice, "This Land Is Your Land," in breaking, high-pitched voices.

The two grown-ups clapped until their hands were sore. "Terrific, boys, just terrific! You're really going to make those children happy tomorrow."

"Will we go right into the hospital?" Adam asked in awe. He'd never been anywhere near a hospital.

"Yes, right in, Adam. They have a special playroom for the children who aren't too sick, and we'll set up the stage in there. In fact," Gilly said, turning toward Mary, "I think I'll pack this stuff in the station wagon today. It will cut down on time tomorrow."

Mary nodded. "That's fine, Gilly. Come, boys, we'll all help, and just *maybe* we'll have time left over for those brownies I made this morning!"

"Mom," Timmy hissed from behind the curtain.

Gilly excused herself from a group of nurses and wound her way through the maze of wheelchairs to the Den Seven Puppet Theater spread across the front of the crowded room.

"Mom, he's still not here . . . and he's two turkeys and the father pilgrim!"

Gilly looked nervously at her watch. It was nearly time

167

to start, but she couldn't bear to begin without Adam. He'd poured himself heart and soul into this production. "Let's hold off for just a minute, Timmy. I'll call." And she dashed off in search of a phone.

Mary answered on the first ring, her voice strained and low. "Hello."

"Mary? It's Gilly. Where's Adam? We're about to start and he's not—"

"Dear, you'll have to go on without him. Adam won't be coming."

Gilly's heart skipped a beat. "Is he all right? Is he ill, Mary?"

"No, Adam's health is fine. I can't explain now, Gilly, but Joe returned this morning, and when he found out where Adam was going, he . . . he decided he'd prefer Adam not be a part of it. . . ."

"Not come?" Gilly's voice echoed off the polished hospital walls.

"I'm sorry, dear."

"Mary"—Gilly gripped the phone until her knuckles were shiny and white—"Mary, can't you do something?"

Mary was silent. Finally she spoke. "No, Gilly. This was Joe's decision. I can't . . . I can't interfere."

"Mary"—Gilly felt tears spring to her eyes—"Adam *has* to come. Mary, you know how much this means to him."

There was pain in Mary's voice and the lilt was gone. "Believe me, Gilly, I know."

"Let me talk to Joe!" Gilly's stomach twisted into painful knots.

"He's not here. He took Adam out."

"Oh, Mary . . . Mary, *why* did Joe do this?"

"Gilly, go back to the boys. They need you now. Try to put this out of your mind, and don't worry about Adam. We'll talk later."

She dropped the phone and stood leaning against the

cool wall. Nothing fit together. She just couldn't understand what Joe was doing to his son.

In a daze she returned to the stage, rearranged parts for eight puzzled little boys, and stood off to the side while the boys entertained a roomful of sparkling, eager children.

After the turkeys' third curtain call the boys tumbled into the audience, eyes bright with success, joking and laughing and making new friends until finally Gilly was able to pull them away, take down the theater, and leave the hospital.

It had been a huge success for everyone—for the boys, for the hospital, for the children. But Gilly felt only the sad disappointment that she knew must be filling Adam Bennett, her dear little friend Adam.

"Timmy, I'd like to stop at the Bennetts' before we go home," she announced after the last scout had been dropped off at his front door. "Is that okay with you?"

"Sure, Mom! I can tell Adam how great we were! Bet he was worried about how we'd handle his puppets. But I think we did okay. Except when Stanley tried to put the turkey on the same hand as the pilgrim."

Gilly nodded, her thoughts elsewhere. "You did great, Tim."

As she drove up the long driveway to the Bennetts' home, Gilly spotted the van off to the side of the house and Joe's small sports car parked in the circle drive. Good. Everyone must be home.

Mary met them at the door. "Gilly dear." She kissed her lightly on the cheek, then pressed Timmy close. "Adam is upstairs, Timmy, and will be anxious to talk to you about the show. Run along up, dear, and I'll join you in a minute, if I may, to hear every single detail!" She pointed him toward the wide staircase, and Timmy ran off happily.

"Is Adam all right, Mary?" Gilly kept her voice low.

"He's disappointed, certainly, but he'll be all right. Children have a resiliency, my dear, that I envy sometimes."

"And Joe?"

Mary's fine brows drew together for a moment, then relaxed into the soft mesh of wrinkles that lined her face. She looked like she wanted to say something, but held back at the last, simply nodding toward the den. "Joseph is in the den."

"I'd like to talk to him, Mary. Would you mind terribly if we took a ride and left the boys here for the rest of the day?"

Mary hugged her. "I wouldn't mind that one single bit. There's still some daylight left. Go, off with you." She turned to go up the stairs, then paused and looked back toward Gilly.

"And Gilly?"

"Yes, Mary."

"Remember how very much he loves you."

Gilly smiled sadly and went to find Joe.

There was no anger this time, no harsh words, only a poignant sadness that filtered through the air as Gilly headed her car north toward the open fields of Bucks County.

Joe sat beside her, his long legs stretched out amid the McDonald's wrappers, baseballs, and long-forgotten school papers that cluttered the floor. His hands were clasped behind his head, his eyes half closed.

Leaving the congestion of the city behind them, Gilly pulled off the highway onto a quiet country road and drove slowly along, drinking in the solitude of the rolling fields and blue sky. Each of them seemed lost in reflections, pulling out thoughts, touching upon them gently, then tucking them back into place until the time was right.

"It's all very confusing, isn't it, Gilly, this business called love."

She nodded quietly. Confusing . . . and painful . . . and complicated . . . and so many other things.

An Amish farmer drove by in his horse-drawn buggy and nodded to them, putting a finger to the brim of his tall black hat. Gilly nodded back, then watched him in her mirror until he disappeared from sight, envying the peace that seemed to move slowly along with him.

Pulling into a small turnaround she switched the engine off and turned toward Joe. "Would you like to walk?"

Joe nodded and they walked along a field, side by side, not touching, their eyes wandering from fields to rambling whitewashed farmhouses that seemed stopped in time.

"Joe, we need to talk." Her eyes focused on a pair of Amish boys playing on a stack of hay in the distance.

"Yes, Gilly, we do."

"I'm not sure about the boat, Joe. I'm not sure at all it can weather those storms."

Pain flashed across Joe's eyes, but he kept his voice steady. "It's our damn minds, Gilly, the way we think. It's your need to be independent, my need to protect, to secure those I love in a safety net. It's . . . it's our cursed philosophies of life, Gilly. They keep muddling things up."

"Yes, Joe," she said quietly, "they do." They had stopped walking, and Gilly now proceeded to a neat, rough-hewn log fence and rested her arms over the top. "I've tried so very hard, Joe, but I don't understand how you think, why you do things."

"Do you understand my love for you?"

Gilly looked out over the field, then back to meet the deep, dark eyes that filled her dreams. "Yes, my dear Joe, that I understand, if one can understand love. And you

171

know I love you." Her voice had dropped to a whisper. "But, Joe, is that enough? Is that enough if we keep moving through life along different paths, moving to different rhythms, being on different sides of the fence every time we turn around?" She felt an overwhelming sadness growing within her.

Beside her Joe was tense, his dark eyes focusing on something millions of miles away.

Gilly looked back out over the countryside and she pointed to a horse-drawn tractor tilling a distant field. "Life doesn't need to be so complicated, Joe, so full of protective shields. Look what it's like out here—you plow, you sow, you harvest. You live, you love, you die. . . ."

She could feel the tension in every muscle of Joe's body, but it didn't prepare Gilly for the anguish she saw when she looked into his eyes. His face was nearly colorless, stark, every muscle rigid, his jaw clenched painfully.

"Joe . . ." Gilly put out a hand to touch him, suddenly afraid.

Nothing moved but his head as he slowly turned it toward her. His hands clenched the rough wood, his fingers straining white against it. "Simple? No, Gilly, life isn't that way at all, don't you see?" His voice was deep and racked with pain. "Sometimes you don't live at all. . . ."

Joe leaned over the fence, his head dipping down between his broad, hunched shoulders. "Nathan didn't live to love, to plow or harvest. . . ." His voice was ragged, the words torn cruelly from his heart. "Nathan didn't even live to say his first words. Nathan died, Gilly, died when he was eleven months old! My son, my firstborn son, torn from me before he ever had a chance to live." Salty tears flowed down his cheeks now, his shoulders shaking in a grief not yet spent. "And I was helpless. I couldn't do a damn thing to save him!"

Gilly's gasp went unheard. Her arm went instinctively around him. "Oh, Joe, no . . ." Her heart filled with an unbearable pain, her mind full of unshakable images of Joe's tiny son, dying.

Joe seemed to find a new energy in the painful out-pouring of the past that had never left him. "He looked so much like Adam—huge brown eyes, and my mother's smile. He was handsome. Smart! A perfect baby boy. Un-til they discovered the kidney problem."

Gilly looked into his face and saw the vacant stare that was seeing things she could never imagine. A parent's most dreaded nightmare, worst agony—the death of a child. Tears clouded her vision and she wiped them away with the back of her hand. "Joe, I'm so sorry." Her choked whisper barely touched him.

"We had Adam, born of grief maybe, but he became my reason for going on. He became my life."

"And Patricia?"

"It was far too late to salvage anything there. She went off and started a new life, and Adam and I survived to-gether. And I vowed then"—he slammed a fist against the fence so hard that tiny shards of wood danced through the air—"I vowed that I would never, *never,* be in a helpless position again, I would never let Adam down like I did Nathan." He swallowed hard, his temple throbbing beneath the tan skin.

"No, Joe, don't say that! Don't *think* that! You didn't let your baby down. You couldn't—"

"I *did,* Gilly!" His voice was harsh and sharp. "I did . . . Nathan died because his father . . ."—the words were forced out, one by one, in painful slowness—"his father couldn't afford the kidney transplant that would have saved his life! I'm the reason, Gilly, I'm the reason my baby died."

Gilly stood in stunned silence. The enormity of what

Joe had carried in his heart all these years slowly seeped into her consciousness.

Joe looked at her, his eyes wet with tears. "Me, Gilly." And then, for the first time since he'd said good-bye to the tiny lifeless form at Children's Hospital, Joe Bennett filled the air with the heart-wrenching, ragged sounds of a man's weeping.

Gilly wrapped her arms around his heaving chest and held him close, murmuring soft words. She didn't ever want to let go. And with tears streaming freely down her cheeks she cried with him for the loss that had torn out a piece of his heart.

A long time later they began to walk again along the path beside the fence. Joe rubbed his hand across his eyes, then looked down at Gilly from swollen sockets, and walked on.

She felt the weight of his look with a heavy heart. So many things moved slowly into focus for the first time. So many bits of conversation rushed back from the folds of her memory and took on meaning. *Joe's incredibly successful business, his need for money to protect his tiny family; his preoccupation with Adam's safety.* Tears stung her eyes as she thought back to his fear the night her car had broken down—a fear he seemed to live with each day. *And the hospital field trip . . . Now it made sense, his shielding Adam from the cruel realities of life, the overwhelming sadness he suffered when Nathan lay in that hospital dying.* She shook her head and tried to fit everything into place, tried to tell herself it would be all right, they could deal with it now. But a cruel, frightening voice deep down inside her said otherwise.

"Joe," she said softly, looking up into his strong, pale face. "Joe, why didn't you tell me about Nathan before?"

He was silent for a long time, his eyes on the path ahead. He shoved his hands deep into his pockets and spoke reluctantly. "I've never talked to anyone about Nathan since the day he died."

"Joe!"

"It was too hard, the wound was too deep. And now it's a damn, bleeding chasm all over again."

"No, Joe, you're wrong. It's not! Maybe now you can deal with it better. You need to let your grief run its course—and maybe you'll be able to see things more clearly."

"What kind of things, Gilly?" His voice had an edge to it.

Gilly searched his face to see what he was feeling. "Things like 'philosophies of life,' Joe," she said kindly. "Things like that—and Adam . . ."

The tears were gone now, and Joe was left with only the pain, and the firm conviction that he would live his life making sure that he never let Adam down, never let him be hurt. His words were hollow and sad. "No, Gilly."

She looked sorrowfully into his eyes. "No?"

"It's the way it is, the way *I* am, don't you see?"

Gilly got back in the car and started the engine, fighting back the tears that stung her eyes. They didn't speak again until she pulled up in the familiar drive, in front of the house she was coming to love.

"Joe . . ." She reached out and touched his arm.

"Why does life do this to us, Gilly?" He turned toward her, his heart full of love and pain and sadness. "But it can't take some things away . . . my memories of Nathan when he smiled at me"—he leaned over and kissed Gilly gently—"or the love I have for you. It will always be here, Gilly, no matter what. Good-bye, Gilly."

Before Gilly could respond, he'd slid out of the car and into the house, leaving the front door open. She sat glued to the seat, her heart throbbing beneath the thin wall of her chest. She wanted to call after him, to throw open the door, to say it didn't matter, she'd raise Adam and Timmy any way he wanted. But she couldn't. And Joe couldn't.

When Timmy appeared minutes later, his blue eyes twinkling happily and his face shadowed with chocolate cake, she mustered a smile from some shadowy hollow, and without a backward glance that might possibly be the end of her, Gilly drove off into the twilight.

CHAPTER FOURTEEN

Gilly stumbled across the dark room and reached for a sweater to stop the chill. Wrapping it tightly around her, over her nightgown and her robe, she walked to the window and stared out into the cold blackness of the night. But what she saw, instead of night, were faces. Timmy . . . Adam . . . Joe . . . She reached out and placed her palm flat against the cold windowpane, wanting to touch him, to pull him back into her life.

Would she ever be warm again? Would the empty hole inside of her ever be filled?

At last morning came, and Gilly groped her way into another joyless day.

"Mrs. Lewandowski sent this up with Timmy today." Tugg shoved the pie in front of Gilly's nose. "Come on, Gilly, you've got to eat something!"

Gilly smiled weakly. "Thanks. Maybe later."

"Holmes, if you want my advice—"

"Did I say that?" Gilly laid her hand across her forehead and tried to ease the pain above her eyebrows.

"Did you say that? Gilly, you've said seventeen, maybe eighteen words in the past four days! Hell, no, you didn't ask for it, but that's never stopped me before!"

"Tugg, I'm sorry." Gilly fought back the tears. Where did they all come from? she wondered vaguely. So many, many tears. She hoped she would run out soon. When the tears stopped, maybe the pain would lessen. "I'm going for a bike ride, Tugg."

"In the middle of the morning? It's freezin' out there!" He looked up from a display of photographs and his voice softened at the look on her face. "Sure, Gilly. Go ahead. I'll take care of things here." He watched her as she pulled a heavy jacket over her thin frame and walked out the door.

The answer was so clear to Tugg. Why couldn't Gilly or Joe see it? Sure, everyone had problems . . . but the strength of Gilly's feelings could slay dragons! Surely it could solve other things. . . . Tugg shook his head and went back to work, trying to dispel the sadness that filled the studio.

Gilly stepped out on the porch and welcomed the icy wind that whipped through her hair. *At least I know I'm still alive,* she thought, feeling her cheeks turn bright red.

As she swung her leg over the bike, she looked automatically to the curb, seeing Joe's car, Joe's smiling face, as clearly as she saw the thin, leafless branches of the maple tree beside the walkway.

"Oh, Joe," she murmured to the mirage, "I love you so very much. . . . I'm so empty without you. What can we do about this, Joe? I thought I could do it, I thought it was best for Adam and Timmy. . . . But there *has* to be another answer, doesn't there?"

She rode on down the street, her head filled with thoughts of Joe's life, the things that had molded this

178

powerful man, the cruel sadness he had endured. Why hadn't he ever talked to anyone about Nathan before? Why hadn't he allowed the pain to be released, to be shared? Why?

"Good morning, Gilly!" Mrs. Lewandowski's shrill voice cut through the air.

Gilly looked up to the porch and waved. "Thanks for the pie, Ida. As usual, it's terrific."

"Well, sweetie, I think I'll send another one tomorrow, try to fatten you up a little. What's happening to you?" She shoved her hands onto her hips and frowned down at Gilly.

"Oh, Tugg and I have been working hard, that's all." Gilly forced a smile and stuck her foot out to the sidewalk to balance the bike.

Ida wrapped her heavy coat about her and trundled down the four porch steps until she stood in front of Gilly's bike. "Don't work too hard, Gilly. Life will pass you by and then what?"

Then what? Yes, then what. Life *was* passing her by, slowly, painfully, and the "then" was an unspeakable agony. She only nodded.

"Well, I've wonderful news that will perk you up, Gilly."

"Good, Ida. Tell me."

"You know my son, my Frank?"

Gilly nodded. She'd never met Frank, but she'd heard many things about him, how he had such a wonderful job, such a good life. A life, Gilly knew sadly, that didn't have any room in it for Ida. He never visited, wrote so rarely his letters became neighborhood events.

"He's coming for Thanksgiving! To be with me." Ida's round face was heavenly, her eyes moist. "He called me and said, 'Mother, I want to be with you. I love you, and I don't want to spend my life separated from people I love.' That's what he said, Gilly." Tears ran down Ida

179

Lewandowski's plump cheeks. "Yes, Gilly dear"—she covered Gilly's hands on the handlebars and shook her head—"my son Frank is coming for one of my cherry pies. He used to love them when he was a boy, you know."

Gilly shook her head, fighting back the tears. "Ida, I'm so happy for you. That's wonderful news—be sure you bring him down." And she hurried on down the street, thoughts of prodigal sons and life's shortness squeezing out the tears.

Four days . . . four days without Joe in her life was the worst torment she had ever been through. Timmy was ready to trade her in, Tugg must be at his wit's end, and she was miserable! What would the rest of her life be like without him? She couldn't imagine it, not in any tiny, infinitesimal way could she imagine it. She could imagine problems with Joe, and difficult times working them out; heaven knows, they'd already been through some of that. She could imagine arguments, she could imagine lovely times of making up, she could imagine Joe pressed in her arms and her life. But the other? Life without him? No, *that* she couldn't begin to imagine! Everything that went to make up Gilly Holmes warred against the very thought. No, life without Joe was unimaginable!

She never felt the stares of the drivers as she U-turned on one wheel and with lightning speed pedaled back home, hardly felt the steps beneath her feet as she flew up to the porch, threw the front door open, and raced into the studio.

Tugg jumped up. "Gilly!"

"Yes, Gilly!" She rushed over and hugged him, squishing his beard between them. "I love him, Tugg! And I'm not giving up."

"Of course you love him!" He hugged her back, a huge smile lighting his face. "And it's only taken four miserable days for you to get smart and go for it!"

180

Gilly tipped up her chin. "Some of us are slower than others. But there's no stopping me now!" Her eyes glowed with loving purpose.

"Need any help?"

Gilly smiled warmly. "Yep. Will you be here for Tim when he gets out of school? And tell him—"

"Don't worry about that. I won't have any trouble figuring out what to tell him!"

Gilly pressed her finger into the doorbell again. Somebody had to be home! She looked anxiously at the door. Joe's secretary said he hadn't been in all week and she didn't know where he was, which, she added worriedly, wasn't like Mr. Bennett at all. *Oh, please, somebody be home!*

Just as she was about to turn back to the car, the door opened. "Gilly!" Mary's arms were around her in a second, her warm body pulling Gilly inside. "Oh, my dear, how very happy I am to see you!"

"Gilly!" Adam tore out of the den at the sound of her voice and threw his arms around her waist. "Hi . . ." His brown eyes looked up, showing embarrassment at his display of affection.

"Hey"—Gilly looked down and hugged him back— "how did you know hugs are my favorite greeting?" She noticed his plaid bathrobe. "Adam, are you sick?" She looked quickly at Mary.

From her spot behind Adam Mary shook her head no before answering, "Well, Adam's been feeling just a little under the weather and thought maybe a day home with me in front of the fire would help."

Gilly looked down and tousled his hair. Of course he was feeling under the weather. And she and Joe had put that feeling there, right smack in the middle of Adam *and* Timmy! They had seen the love that passed between her and Joe—it flowed thicker than honey, of course

181

they'd seen it. And Adam knew he was somehow included in that love. Now, suddenly, his little life was all a shambles again. A surge of anger at herself churned furiously in Gilly's stomach.

"Where's your dad?" Gilly tipped up Adam's chin.

"Did you come to see him?" Adam's brown eyes looked at her carefully.

"Yep, sure did. I think he likes hugs, too, so I thought I'd come and give him one."

Adam's eyes shone. "Yeah, he could *really* use one, Gilly. That's a great idea!"

"But I have to find him first." She looked up at Mary.

Mary shook her head. "Gilly, he isn't here. He . . . he went off for a few days."

"Off? Where?" A sliver of fear sliced through her.

"Well, it's confidential, but—"

"But not from Gilly, Gram!" Adam stuck his small body between them.

Mary looked down at her grandson and smiled. "You're absolutely right. Not from Gilly. She's family." Her eyes moved quickly back to Gilly's face to catch the grin she knew would be there. She pressed Gilly's hand firmly, lovingly, in her own.

"Gilly, there's a small inn west of here. Alan, Joe's father, used to take him there now and again when he was a boy. It was always special to Joe, peaceful. He didn't want anyone to know where he was, but"—she smiled at Gilly—"but Joe needs you very much right now, Gilly."

Mary bent over the small table to write down the directions. Adam, pleased that his day seemed put back together, hugged Gilly once more, and ran back to the den to watch cartoons.

Mary handed her the piece of paper and walked with Gilly to the door. "Gilly, if you go to him . . ."

Gilly looked at her long, reading the unspoken words.

"Yes, I know, Mary. If I go to him, I can't walk away again. I don't want to *ever* be away from him again, Mary. Never!"

Mary's eyes glistened. "Does that mean I can start packing?"

Gilly smiled. "Definitely not. At least not until our first Thanksgiving dinner together."

Mary nodded, dabbing at her moist eyes. "Yes. So much to be thankful for, my dear. Now go and you'll be there before dark. And drive carefully, Gilly." She opened the door and gently guided Gilly out, then stood for a long time on the porch, staring out into her son's future that was finally beginning, at last.

The inn was easy to find, set back from the road in a nest of old maple trees. Gilly's heart leapt clear up to her throat as she turned into the drive. Joe! Joe was only minutes away. . . .

She'd gone over and over what she was going to say to him, how they'd handle their differences, how they'd work through things, how nothing else in this whole world made any sense without him!

Her step light and a bounce to her walk, she flew into the inn.

A white-haired gentleman stood behind the desk and watched the lovely, rosy-cheeked lady approach. *Ah, to be young,* he thought with a smile. She had that kind of flashing light in her eyes that could move mountains, an on-top-of-the-world grin that lit her whole face.

Gilly came to a stop before him, her hair spilling over one shoulder. "Mr. Joe Bennett, please. I think he's a guest here?"

The man registered surprise. The pretty, loose-haired woman's look surely didn't match the sadness that filled the deep eyes of the fellow in 101. He shook his head. Well, maybe she was some kind of medicine. He sure looked like he needed some. "Sure is, ma'am." He smiled. "But I do believe he's out taking a stroll right now. The back door's thataway if you'd care to look for him. He couldn't be far."

Gilly nodded her thanks and crossed the cozy lobby and out onto a sweeping, open back-porch.

Her heart stopped. Joe stood at the fence, his back to her, his broad shoulders outlined clearly against the fading light. He was looking off across a rolling meadow, the wind sweeping his black hair back, a thick fisherman's sweater keeping out the cold. But he didn't seem to notice the cold, or the meadow. He stood so still Gilly's breath caught in her throat.

And then he turned, almost as if she had touched him with her look. He turned and stared at the woman standing on the old whitewashed porch, her hair whipping about her lovely face, her eyes loving him.

"Gilly." The single word tore from Joe's throat, and she covered the distance between them in a single second, throwing herself into his arms, wrapping her arms around his neck as if she'd never, ever, let go.

"Oh, Joe"—tears stopped her words as Gilly looked up into his eyes, a smile tipping her lips—"I didn't think I had any tears left!" She released one hand from his neck and wiped them away.

"Gilly, I love you, I love you, I love you. . . ." Joe murmured, holding her a space apart to soak in every inch of her.

"We can do it, Joe. We *can.*"

He pulled her close again, not believing she was really there, cradled against his heart where she belonged. "Oh, Gilly . . ." There were so many questions, so many things to say, and all he could do was repeat her name, his love for her. Finally, with great effort, he pulled apart and sought her eyes.

"Gilly, there are things we need to say."

She nodded, loving him. "Yes, Joe. But no matter what we say, no matter what there is ahead, I know, more surely than I've ever known anything in my life, that we can deal with it. Together, Joe . . . together we can work it out."

Joe brushed her hair back, loving the silky feel of it against his hand, then held her close. "Gilly, being here alone, thinking and aching—I've come up with some starts, at least." He kissed her hair. "I was hurting and angry when I came, angry at me, at life, at you for tearing open the wound, the memories . . ."

Gilly tilted her head back and watched him quietly, her eyes searching his face.

". . . and I realized, sometime in the middle of that first sleepless night"—he smiled softly—"that I told you about Nathan because you had reached that part of me— had put up with me long enough to peel away all the other layers, and that's what was left. I loved you so deeply, and it poured out."

"I only wish I had known sooner, my darling—it explained so many things."

"You don't go through something like that and remain the same, Gilly. Patricia lost herself in travel and excitement, I built a coat of armor around Adam and me. I knew I could never endure such pain again. Until you and I parted. . . ."

"See?" Gilly ran a finger over his cheeks, traced the wonderful line of his lips. "The armor wasn't foolproof. I sneaked in."

He kissed her gently. "Sneaked in, but it almost drove you away. My sweet, free-spirited Gilly . . . don't ever leave me, my darling."

Pushing her head back, her eyes shining with love, she looked into his ebony eyes. "Not a chance, Mr. Bennett, not a chance." Her laughter was music on the wind whipping around them. "I came loaded down with arguments—"

"Already? We're not even married yet!"

"No, silly"—she hushed him with a kiss—"arguments to convince you we could work out our differences, that we could raise Adam and Timmy in harmony—" Her voice broke off and she stared at him. "Married! Joe, you haven't asked—"

"Me? My independent, spirited Gilly, I was waiting for you—"

She reached up and held his head between her hands, a loving smile spreading from her eyes to his face. "Joe Bennett, I love you. Will you marry me?"

Joe wrapped his arms around her, then lifted her off the ground, spinning her around and around and around, sealing his answer in a dizzying swirl of love.

JAYNE CASTLE

excites and delights you with tales of adventure and romance

___

____TRADING SECRETS

Sabrina had wanted only a casual vacation fling with the rugged Matt. But the extraordinary pull between them made that impossible. So did her growing relationship with his son—and her daring attempt to save the boy's life.
19053-3-15 $3.50

____DOUBLE DEALING

Jayne Castle sweeps you into the corporate world of multimillion dollar real estate schemes and the very private world of executive lovers. Mixing business with pleasure, they made *passion* their bottom line.
12121-3-18 $3.95